Nullo

In a hellhole of a prison in the fever-ridden jungles south of the border, the gringo called Nullo gambles a handful of smuggled gold on his cellmate's plan of escape. The kid, Jamie, goes free but before he can spring Nullo, all hell breaks loose. A bloody riot ends in a mass breakout and Nullo finds himself fleeing in the company of the most dreaded bandit in the country, the albino monster known as El Blanco.

Leaving horror and anguish in its wake, the gang ride for Jamie's farm where Blanco believes there is a heap of gold for the taking. There the stage is set for a scene of tension and suspense that culminates in tragedy when Jamie's beautiful wife dies – at the hands of Nullo.

What follows is a bizarre and bloody tale of vengeance where motives are suspect and no man is quite what he seems.

Nullo

JACK GALLAGHER

A Black Horse Western

ROBERT HALE · LONDON

00253198

ISBN 0 7090 7147 7

Robert Hale Limited
Clerkenwell House
Clerkenwell Green
London EC1R 0HT

Typeset by
Derek Doyle & Associates, Liverpool.
Printed and bound in Great Britain by
Antony Rowe Limited, Wiltshire.

One

Trouble. Maybe with a knife. Jaime Vargas didn't want no trouble.

There were three of them in the cell. Four if you counted the spider. The spider was as big as a woman's hand and it clung to the adobe wall near the nine-inch-square hole that served as a window. It had a settled look, as if it meant to bide its time till hell froze. Jaime sat on a sawdust-stuffed mattress on the floor by the wall. The bunks were taken up by the two *Norteamericanos*.

The man on the top bunk, Tibbs, was occupied in scraping a knife along a piece of Arkansas stone. Every time the guard's footsteps sounded, he would hide the knife and the stone. When the guard had gone he would take them out again and continue to scrape. With the heat, the smell of the night soil pail in the corner and the scraping of the knife, Jaime thought he would go crazy.

He wished the man on the bottom bunk would

say something. The silence was an insult to the man on the top bunk, Jaime could tell. He had been here first, he was very big and ugly and he had a knife, so it was up to the newcomer to talk and try to win his friendship. But he said nothing, just lay on his bunk and played with a limp looking pack of cards. Jaime kept his mouth shut too. As far as they were concerned he did not speak English.

Jaime did not want any trouble. All he wanted was his beautiful Mescalero wife. But if Tibbs made trouble with him he would have to fight. He was no tough guy, but he wanted to feel good with his wife, if he ever saw her again. A tough guy was somebody who liked trouble. The man on the bottom bunk was a tough guy. He could keep his mouth shut and not even think he was looking for trouble, but he was looking for it all right.

'Stinking heat,' Tibbs said.

Jaime waited for the man on the bottom bunk to say something. He just shuffled his cards and said nothing and Jaime felt his nerves stretch with the tension. Jaime scratched at the heat rash on his chest and muttered something in Spanish.

'I can stomach the heat and I can stomach the smell of shit, but I'm damned if I can stomach the company,' Tibbs said. 'Never could stand tedious company. Yes, I like my men happy and humorous and downright gabby. What you say, *cholo*?' Jaime told himself the word '*cholo*' was just a word mixed up with a lot of English words and he could easily miss it if he knew no English. But his face darkened and Tibbs sneered. Tibbs craned his head over the bunk.

'You been down in Chihuahua?'

The man in the bottom bunk said nothing and Tibbs frowned.

'Yeah, I know you been in Chihuahua. I been speaking with that little cripple Porfirio. Por-feeree-o,' Tibbs repeated and shook his head. 'The gimp was in Chihuahua when they struck gold digging the millrace. He knows you from there. He remembers that buckskin shirt . . . and the fancy buttons.'

Jaime looked at the buckskin shirt. It was fine, soft buckskin without any beads or fringes, but the buttons were not fancy. They were big and black and not really a good match for the pale buckskin.

'I hear you won that shirt and them buttons in a card game in Chihuahua. I hear you put up a regular heap of dollars against that shirt. That right?'

The man in the bottom bunk said nothing and Tibbs gave a slow hard grind at his stone.

Two strokes of that Arkansas will put an edge on a knife, Jaime thought. He will be lucky if he has any blade left by the time he finishes with it.

'A greaser and a bore.'

Jaime sunk his head in his chest and pretended to sleep.

The bunk groaned loudly and Jaime opened his eyes a crack. Tibbs rolled his legs off the bunk. He sat for a moment with his big belly resting on his thighs, then he lowered one foot on to the bottom bunk and stepped down. He walked over and grabbed the bars and stood looking morosely at the adobe wall opposite the cell. He craned his big square head over his shoulder and stared at the man on the bottom bunk.

Jaime looked through his eyelashes at the man, watching to see how he made out under Tibbs's stare. He continued shuffling the cards. He did a fancy riffle and Jaime thought either he was not bothered at all by Tibbs or he had iron self-control.

'I feel like a game of cards,' Tibbs said. 'What have you got to bet?'

Jaime's eyes opened wide at the sound of the man's voice.

'I'll give you my IOU.'

'No bet.'

'Something wrong with my marker?'

'I don't know.'

'I got scum under my armpit. It smells high and rancid. How about if I play you for that?'

'The *cuchillo*.'

'You want my knife?'

'Yeah.'

'What have you got to bet against my knife?'

'This buckskin shirt is what I got. All but the buttons.'

'It's the buttons I want.'

'I know you want the buttons, *amigo*.'

'Yeah, I want them buttons, *amigo*. Let's play.'

Tibbs went down on his hunkers, took the pack of cards out of the man's hand and began to shuffle.

'You got a name?'

'Don't worry about my name.'

'What is it – Aloysius?'

'That's right.'

Tibbs chuckled. 'That's right. OK, Aloysius, five-card draw.'

Jaime knew the man's name. It was Nullo. He had heard Porfirio call him that, and Tibbs had too. Whether it was his real name or just a nickname picked up in Chihuahua, he did not know.

Tibbs dealt the cards. He studied his hand and changed one card. Nullo changed three cards and Tibbs's eyes brightened.

'Two pair. Jacks and tens.'

Tibbs threw his hand on the floor.

Nullo threw down two deuces. He threw down another deuce and Tibbs grinned. Nullo threw down the fourth deuce and Tibbs grinned wider still. His grin was so wide you could see a couple of side teeth were missing.

'I'll take the *cuchillo*.'

Tibbs was grinning but Jaime could see he was not happy. Now it comes, Jaime thought. If this Tibbs meekly handed over the knife, Jaime would be as surprised as if he should get up on his toes and dance the dance of the lovesick faun. And now Nullo was in danger of looking stupid. If Tibbs did not hand over the knife, what was he going to do? Take it off him? Handling trouble when someone brings it to you is one thing, but it is another thing to bring trouble to someone else.

'You want to give it to me?'

Tibbs got up and leaned against the bars of the cell. He took the knife out of his shirt pocket and opened the blade.

'You want the knife?'

'That's right.'

Tibbs looked at the knife. 'This knife here?'

'That's right.'

'That's right. I'll give it to you in the liver, how about that? How about I pop your gut-bag? Like to feel the hot bile scald your tripes?'

'Keep the knife, *amigo*.'

Tibbs laughed. 'Keep the knife, *amigo*.'

Tibbs couldn't think what to say next so he laughed again. He leaned against the bars of the cell, fingering the knife and looking at Nullo. He was grinning and his mind was working.

Nullo sighed. 'I'm going to call you asshole from now on.'

Tibbs stopped grinning. 'Say again?'

'You heard, asshole. It's nothing personal, asshole. See, you figure I backed down over the knife. It's true, I did. But you won't let it rest. You'll want to see me running scared next. Well, the way I figure is: you keep the knife, and I call you asshole.'

'Maybe I don't like being called asshole.'

'You're a fat asshole.'

Nullo got up from the bunk.

'You got a worried look. Desperadoes don't worry. It's damn the consequences.'

A slow grin spread over Tibbs's face. 'You're all right,' he said. 'Here, here's your knife.'

Tibbs held out the knife. Nullo kept his hands by his side.

'Why don't you take it?' As he spoke Tibbs lunged and Nullo doubled over the knife so that Jaime Vargas – jumping to his feet to avoid them – couldn't see if Nullo had been stuck or not.

The next thing Jaime knew, Tibbs bumped him with his belly into the corner. Tibbs's big face was right in front of his, his eyes were wide and fixed but they didn't see Jaime. Tibbs pushed himself off and began to turn. But Nullo didn't let him turn. He gave Tibbs a rabbit punch and grabbed his knife-hand. Tibbs's shirtsleeve tore in Nullo's hand. Nullo went after the knife-hand again before Tibbs could turn, and locked two hands round the wrist. Tibbs tried to turn, and Nullo didn't try to stop him. He let him wheel round in

a circle like a man who has a wildcat by the tail.
Tibbs grabbed one of the bars of the cell with his
left hand. To Jaime Vargas it was like Nullo had
rehearsed his next move about a hundred times –
instead of thinking it up on the spur of the
moment. Still gripping Tibbs's knife-hand, he slid
in behind him, slapped his back flat against
Tibbs's. He lifted a boot and braced it against one
of the cell bars. He hauled back on Tibbs's arm
like a boatman hauling on a stiff tiller. Tibbs
wanted to keep his right arm attached to his
shoulder, so he let go of the cell bar. As soon as he
did, Nullo shoved hard against the bar with his
bracing foot and Jaime had to dive into the
bottom bunk to avoid being crushed into the
corner by Tibbs.

The wind was knocked out of Tibbs. Jaime
heard it burp out of his gullet when his belly hit
the wall. While he was groggy, Nullo kicked his
feet away and brought him to his knees.

Crouching on the bottom bunk, Jaime could not
see Nullo's head, but Tibbs's face was right in
front of him – his cheek was flattened against the
adobe wall so that his mouth pouted like a kid's
when you squeeze its cheeks. Nullo was still hold-
ing Tibbs's knife-hand in both of his and his right
boot was shoved against Tibbs's shoulder blade.

Jaime could see the fight going out of Tibbs.
Tibbs looked right at Jaime – an angry, defiant
look. Jaime thought he'd found the will to fight on.

But Tibbs opened his hand and let the knife fall. He looked away from Jaime's eyes.

'Lemme up, for Christ sake,' he said in a dead, flat voice.

Jaime watched Nullo's boot settle against Tibbs's shoulder blade. Tibbs's eyes opened, turned to the side and up, so that the pupils were almost lost and a lot of bloodshot white was on view. Tibbs strained to see Nullo's face, and Jaime ducked his head and tried to see it too, but Nullo was cut off at the neck by the top bunk and short of poking his head out Jaime couldn't get a look at his face.

For a couple of seconds Tibbs and Nullo were as still as statues. Jaime noticed blood on Nullo's shirt, low down, around the last of the buttons before the waistband of his pants. The black button was nicked or scored and Jaime caught a yellow gleam from it.

Nullo's body started to bend backwards and the leg braced against Tibbs's shoulder began to straighten. Tibbs struggled. Blood ran out of his pushed-open mouth. Tibbs moaned and Jaime heard a sound that made him think of how it sounds when you begin breaking the leg of a roast chicken.

Jaime scrambled out of the bunk. He felt as light as a feather. He felt his eyes were flickering from side to side as fast as a vibrating guitar string. The memory of that snapping sound made him very queasy.

'What's wrong with him?'

Nullo looked at him. Jaime couldn't read human feeling or motive in his eyes. He felt a fear that was primitive, that he felt in his organs and his spine. Then Nullo looked away and Jaime said:

'The blood . . .'

'I reckon he bit his tongue,' Nullo said.

'You're hurt.'

Nullo looked at the blood on his shirt.

'I'll live.'

His fingers touched the scored button, turned it, and once again Jaime caught that yellow gleam.

A fancy shirt, with buttons made of gold.

Two

Nullo made a racket with his boot heel on the cell bars until the guard came. Jaime told the guard that Tibbs had fallen off his bunk and broken his arm. The guard did some muttering in his Yaquis dialect. He cuffed Jaime round the ear, and he cast some baleful glances at Nullo, but something about the look of Nullo kept him from laying hands on him. Finally he called another guard and Tibbs was hauled off to the infirmary.

Nullo opened the blade of Tibbs's knife, and Jaime thought: if he gets out that stone and commences to scrape, I will throw back my head and howl like a coyote. Nullo ran his finger along the blade, pressed the point with the ball of his thumb. Then with a motion that was so smooth and relaxed that Jaime forgot to be startled, he flipped the knife and nailed the spider to the wall.

The tip of the blade held in the soft adobe for a few seconds until the wriggling of the spider dislodged it. The skewered spider flopped to the floor and Jaime watched with interest as it scuttled along with the knife sticking up from its back and the tip of the blade making faint scraping sounds on the screed floor.

Nullo picked up the knife and unstuck the spider by drawing the blade against a bar. The spider landed on its back outside the cell, and stayed there waggling its legs every now and then.

Jaime put on a brave face. '*Amigo*, I would be grateful if you would conceal that knife. It is making me nervous.'

'What makes you think you got cause to fear harm from me?'

'It seems to me that every other living creature in your vicinity has come to grief.'

'You speak good English.'

'Thank you. I was taught by a wise and holy man.'

'The spider was a threat. Spiders can bite.'

'This spider would not have bitten.'

'Seems to me you're a trusting soul. Tibbs was a threat too. Tibbs can't live and let live. And he knew I was packing gold.'

'I too know that the buttons of your shirt could furnish a wardrobe for many men.'

'That's true.'

16

'But it seems to me that if both your cell-mates suffered accidents then it would not look good for you.'

'In that case, I reckon I'll take the top bunk. I wouldn't want you to fall out of it.'

'You are very considerate.'

'I know how to live and let live.'

'That is your philosophy, I think.'

'It ain't a bad one.'

'I have a better.'

'Yeah?'

'Yes, because it goes one step further than yours. If we live and let live, it means we are not enemies. My philosophy is: Live and help live. Under my philosophy we become friends.'

'Friends are enemies in the making.'

'If I believed that, I would not want to live.'

Nullo smiled – a bleak-eyed sort of smile.

'I see it will not be easy to convert you to my philosophy, but I believe I can do it. You see, I have an idea.'

Nullo stretched out on the top bunk and closed his eyes. Jaime could not decide if this meant Nullo was terminating the conversation or not. He spoke anyway.

'Let me introduce myself: my name is Jaime Vargas. My father named me after a great liberator named Captain Jamie McTavish, with whom he fought and suffered many hardships in the retreat into the Land of Fire long ago. My mother was a Mescalero Indian. My wife is Mescalero too. The Mescalero are a people of much heart. Poor Maria's heart will be broken when she returns from visiting her family and finds that I have been taken by the *federales*. Ah, Maria, the beautiful child.' Jaime turned away, because his eyes had filled with tears. It was a thing that often happened when he thought of Maria.

'Pretty, huh?'

Jaime squinted out of the corner of his eye. He could not tell if Nullo's eyes were completely closed, or if he squinted back.

'An angel from heaven, my friend.'

'She'll find a man to bring meat to her table.'

Jaime found himself angry with this tough guy – until he remembered that you do not get angry with tough guys.

'Maria . . . you do not know Maria. There's a philosophy in her heart to baffle wise men. She will wait for me, and by hook or by crook I will return to her.'

'Why were you arrested?'

'They accused me of being a rebel. A false accusation.'

'Me too. Are there any genuine rebels in this country?'

'There are some. But they know how to hide. Whenever the rebels cause trouble, the *federales* make arrests. If they cannot find rebels to arrest, they arrest who they can. Arrests look good. They are profitable too. People will pay money to have their loved ones returned to them. The mining companies pay money for the labour of prisoners. A rebel's goods and land can be confiscated – which is the reason I was taken. I was in the field cutting maize when they took me. It will rot on the stalk now. Let it. I would be lucky to get what would feed me for a month out of it. This country is rich – in minerals – in silver and gold and tin. My land is rich in rock. A patch of worthless dirt.'

'But they still aim to confiscate it?'

'Yes, because they think there is gold there. The mining company has discovered gold in the hills above my farm. I got the fever and started to dig too. All I found was some iron pyrites. But the geologist from the mining company became interested and he wanted to have a look at my land. Then, down in the village they started saying to me: "So, Jaime, we hear you have found gold". I denied it, but they did not believe my denials. The geologist from the mining company began to hear rumours that I had struck gold. When he asked me, I told him that if I had struck gold naturally I would have declared it, because it is a crime to keep a strike secret from the government. I could tell he did not believe me. "Let me examine your land, and if there is gold there I will make you an offer for your property," he said. I said: "If you want to buy my property you can make me an offer, but it will have to be a blind offer because I will not let you look at it". And I could see he was thinking: "He thinks if I find his gold he will be at my mercy, because I could threaten to inform on him for mining without permission". But, of course, he was in a dilemma: I could be telling the truth after all and there truly was no gold.'

'Gold is trouble. Even gold that don't exist.'

'There is great power in gold. As you say: in the fact of it, or in the notion of it. I tried to make use of that power – with the consequences you see. Ah, I was trying to prove something. People think I am a fool, and, in trying to prove them wrong by being very cunning, I succeeded in convincing them they are right. Myself, I am not convinced: I think I am not a fool, but only unlucky. And all is not lost – I told you I have an idea.'

'Well, I got ears.'

'Then listen. The geologist from the mining company was wavering. A fish ready to be hooked, and all that was missing was the bait. My friend, now the bait is at hand. In the form of half a dozen shirt buttons.'

'Seems to me there's a flaw in your plan. You can't hook a fish on dry land – and you got to get out of here before you hook that geologist.'

'The gold in those buttons can get us out of here.'

'I thought of that. It wouldn't work. The governor's got a greasy palm, all right, but if a man tells him he's got money, he's liable to take it off him and keep him here.'

`What if we make nuggets of your gold, and tell him it is from my gold mine? That way I could promise him more. He would have to let me go in order to receive the further payment.'

'Where do I come in to this – apart from staking your escape?'

'That is the second part of the plan. When I get home I let the remainder of the gold be seen in the village. The geologist will get to hear that I truly have gold and will be swayed to make me an offer. With the money, I will buy you out of prison.'

'If the governor doesn't take the gold and keep you here – if you can hoodwink the mining company.'

'It is worth a try.'

'If I can trust you to bribe me out. Too many ifs.'

'I swear to you can trust me. Look in my eyes.'

'You might believe what you're saying now, but no man can trust himself from one day to the next.'

'But you must believe in people sometimes in this life. What is it you believe in?'

Nullo lifted a card off the deck on his chest. 'Chance.'

'You are a gambler. Well, gamble on my plan. Gamble on me.'

'You 'mind me of a drummer that sold me a Remington pistol.'

'Was it a good pistol?'

'I seen worse.' Nullo cut the deck again. Jaime could not see what card he had turned up. Nullo looked at it for a few seconds, then he said, 'OK.'

Three

Nullo cut the buttons off his shirt and Jaime
took the knife from him. He began scraping . . .
and scraping . . . and scraping. He used the
sharpening stone too, and when all the black
enamel was off, he cut the buttons into smaller
fragments. So far so good, he decided, but the
pieces of gold did not look like natural nuggets.
They tried pressing them between the bottom of
one of the bunk-legs and the floor, but both the
wood of the leg and the cement of the screed
were too soft. They tried to crush them between
the steel cleats of Nullo's boot heels, but it was
impossible to bring enough pressure to bear.
Finally Nullo had the idea of using the knife. By
placing one of the fragments in near the hinge
and folding the knife, he eventually managed to
distort the gold.

Jaime cut a piece of cotton from the tail of his
peasant's smock and wrapped some of the pieces

in it. The rest he concealed by nicking the waist-band of his pants and pushing the nuggets into the small hole. He worked the nuggets along through the doubled material of the waistband until they were evenly distributed around his waist.

'I feel this plan will be successful,' Jaime said. 'We are both innocent. It is true that I intend to defraud the mining company – this is a dishonest act, but it is not the same as robbing a poor man – really it is nothing. We will succeed because we have right on our side.'

Nullo grinned a sour grin. 'I'd rather have luck on our side.'

'I feel nervous. I fear the governor.'

There was no sympathy or encouragement in Nullo's dead eyes. 'You better worry about me too,' he said. 'If you double-cross me, I'll kill you.'

Jaime's grin gave way to a sullen, baffled look. 'You are my friend.' But his optimistic heart could not be heavy for long. He laughed. 'You will see. I will set you free, then I will make you my friend. I have winning ways, you know.'

'Save them for the governor, kid. Try and act savvy with him. He'll screw you if he thinks you're green.'

'Cut the cards, Nullo. I want to see if I will be lucky.'

'There's no connection.'

'But I think there is.'

Jaime reached for the cards on the bunk. He cut the deck, then froze with the cut facing the floor.

'I am afraid to look. Is it a lucky card?'

Nullo took the half-deck from him. He looked at a single spade.

'There's no second-guessing luck. It doesn't exist till it happens.'

'Is it a good card?'

'It's good. Jack of Diamonds.'

'Jack of Diamonds is my only friend.'

Jaime began to bang on the bars of the cell.

When the Yaquis guard came he swung his key-chain fast enough to give Jaime a bloody knuckle before he could snatch his hands away from the bars. But Jaime pleaded and wheedled, called him 'excellency', begged until eventually the guard's face, with its jumble of chipped tombstones crowding open the thick lips, took on a magnanimous expression and he opened the cell door.

Nullo lay on his bunk. He didn't wonder how Jaime was faring with the governor. It was out of his hands, and no action of his could change the course of events. He forgot about Jaime, forgot about the plan, forgot about everything. His mind emptied. Anyone looking at him would have thought he was asleep. But he heard every sound. Heard the curses and mutterings of the other prisoners. Heard the clink of the guards' chains. Heard the slow rustle of palms in the hot breeze.

Anyone looking at him would have thought his eyes were closed, but when a fly buzzed close to his head he grabbed it out of the air. He thought about the wide-open spaces of the desert.

The dry wheel-hub squealed. Then came a thud as the back legs of the cart hit the ground. A rattle of tin. The axle grated as the wheel began to turn again. The cart came into view and stopped outside the cell. Porfirio lifted a tin pail from a stack and ladled soup into it from a tin tub. He pushed the pail under the bars of the cell, then he dropped a chunk of grey bread between the bars so it splashed in the soup.

'Room service,' Porfirio said. 'Just like the Hotel Nacional. Of course, there you would not have to eat in the smell of your own shit. No, there would most probably be flowers on the table, and certainly no pail of shit. In fact, this is nothing like the Hotel Nacional at all. But no one goes to the mess hall today. There are no guards to spare, you see.'

Nullo stirred the soup with the hunk of bread – there was no spoon – and some bits of spinach-stalk and a few frijole beans broke the scum of the surface.

'Why no guards?'

'They are all looking after our new guest.'

Porfirio limped in between the handles of the cart and lifted. The wheels gave a slow screech as they turned a half-circle. Porfirio squinted sideways at Nullo. When he saw he wasn't going to question him further, he dropped the cart and limped over to the bars of the cell.

'Ah, if you knew who was here, your blood would freeze in your veins.' He looked at Nullo expectantly. 'Is the soup good? The seasoning is personal to the cook. Very personal, you may say. He clears his throat into it. But the cook eats well, and if there is any flavour to the soup, it comes from his spit. Would you like to know who our new guest is?'

'Blanco.'

Porfirio frowned. 'How did you know? Does the Devil whisper secrets in your ear, gringo?'

'You're bold today, gimp.'

'Yes, why should I fear you? When the leopard appears you do not fear the dog. I have only so much fear and it is all for Blanco. He is a drinker of blood. Once, when he caught a party of *federales*, he hung them from a tree – by the neck, with their own guts. Men's screams are music to him.'

'I guess it don't do for a bandit to get a reputation as an easy-going type.'

'Blanco is not cruel for the sake of his reputation. Hate is his religion. I believe it is because he is so ugly. The beautiful feed on love, and the rest must take the leavings. For one so hideous as Blanco, there is nothing left but hate.'

'I guess you know what you're talking about.'

27

'Yes, I am not beautiful.'

'Not hardly.'

'A man must nourish his soul on something. If not love, then hate. Except for you, gringo. I look in your eyes and I understand why men lost in the desert go mad. With those eyes, why has no one killed you before now? Blanco will do it, if you look at him with those eyes. But do I see something in your eyes, after all? Do I see fear?'

'I guess you might, gimp. The thought of swallowing this here slop gets me kind of nervous.'

'I will tell Blanco you do not fear him.'

'You been doing too much talking one way or another. I might have to kill you, you know.'

Nullo said this without menace, conversationally, but Porfirio paled.

'I can't help talking. I am a fool – of the talking kind. But listen – I will not talk about you any more. This I swear.'

Porfirio grabbed the ladle and plunged it into the soup. After some moments of raking about the bottom of the tub he drew out a fish-head with part of the spine attached. He lifted it with his fingers and reached through the bars to drop it in Nullo's soup.

'I was saving it for myself. I have some news you might not have heard. While I was replacing the bucket in the governor's private latrine, I heard it. There will be a scourging tomorrow. The peon from Yautapec who bit off the finger of the

28

guard Juárez. He is to be punished. It is for the benefit of Blanco. The governor wants to show him that he is a hard man. Beside Blanco, the governor is a woman. Once . . . once this man Blanco introduced – through a small incision – a viper into the stomach of his own brother.' Porfirio nodded, bright-eyed. 'Is that not something? However, the viper did not bite, and after some minutes escaped through the mouth. And the brother of Blanco lived. A lucky man. Except, some time after, it is said, his wife baked some fresh bread and served the brother of Blanco a chorizo sausage on a plate. The brother of Blanco screamed – some connection of ideas, you understand – and for a long time continued to scream. And now it is said, he is fed with a spoon, and often crawls upon the ground because he believes he is a beetle.'

Four

The peon had plenty of fight in him. It took three guards to drag him from his cell. The crowd of prisoners made way before the struggling knot of peon and guards – encouraged in this by a fourth guard who went before clubbing with his rifle butt the slow to move. The yells of those who could not push through the press to escape a blow were drowned in the angry clamour of yelling and whistling. The prisoners did not like this use of the whip. The bastinado was bad enough, but it was preferable to a return to the bad old days of flogging.

Nullo found a place under the palm thatch of the kitchen that offered shelter from the cruel noon glare. He did not have this strip of shade to himself though. The stink of sweat from the bodies on each side and the smell of blood from the kitchen, where a fresh hog carcass had been left to drain into a basin, were high and rank.

When he escaped in his mind from this place –
this place that was like a steam bath held in a
madhouse cesspit – it was to the desert his
thoughts took him. He thought about the silent
days in the dry heat. The pure cold of the nights
under the stars glittering like chips of ice. In the
cold nights the camp-fire burned with a dry
crackle, its red flames seared the skin of your face
and hands. No noise, no smell, nothing to trouble
the eye.

The guards manhandled the peon up to the
punishment stake. They pushed his torso against
the stake and tied one end of a rope round his
wrists. A guard with plenty of weight on him took
the other end of the rope and pulled so that the
peon's arms were stretched straight out and chest
and cheek were flattened against the stake. They
pulled his shirt over his head, left it bunched
under his chin. The muscles of his back rippled
under a sheen of sweat. He was young and supple.
The sun caught the smooth flat lines of his temple
and cheekbones and chin, and threw black
shadow over his deep-set eyes.

The governor strode out of his quarters carrying a leather whip coiled in his hand. The governor had big white moustaches that hid his mouth
and swept up along the lines of his jawbone, and
he was wearing his army tunic for the occasion.
He carried himself with chest puffed out and belly
sucked in so that the row of silver buttons made a

smart, soldier-like curve over his torso. He stood before them and held the whip high above his head.

The noise of the prisoners faded a little as they watched the governor standing with his silver buttons glittering in the sun, the coiled whip raised above his head. 'I want to talk to you about humility,' he shouted. He had a good, sonorous voice, and the sense of delivery of a mediocre actor. You could tell he enjoyed making speeches, but the prisoners were not as fond of listening to them and they kept up their chatter while he talked.

'There are wilful men among you. You are all wilful in part. That is why you are here. And here you will learn humility. So that you can live as men among men, and not like animals of the forest. The law of life is to obey. I obey the government, the government obeys the president, and the president obeys God. And you . . . you will obey me. For, by God, I will humble every proud man among you. I will break any wilful spirit that opposes itself to me. I will be to you the scourge of God.'

The governor let the whip uncoil, brought it back over his head and lashed the ground. He was not handy with the whip, and the prisoners laughed. The governor's face betrayed his discomfiture and annoyance. He coiled the whip three times and handed it to the tall, lean, mestizo called Valdez.

The men became quiet for Valdez, as they had not for the governor. Valdez, angular, too wide at the hips and long in the back, moved awkwardly. But the whip came to life in his hand. It uncoiled with the evil grace of a snake. It arched its thin body . . . spat.

In the silence, the echo of that malevolent lash lingered in the dead heat of noonday.

Valdez turned his saturnine face to the peon. He twitched his hand and the whip floated lazily past the peon's back. Valdez stepped back and found his distance and coiled the whip. He looked at the peon and the peon met his eye. The peon's face was set, the lips drawn back showing his clenched teeth very white. The lean-shanked body of Valdez twisted, and his arm came back. The thin black serpent uncoiled.

The eyes of the prisoners, slitted to the noon glare, watched it undulate, looping back, looping forward. It glided swiftly towards the peon, sure, intent, and it hovered . . . drew back. . . . A wave rolled through its body, gathering speed, concentrating its power – then a brief whistle and – CRA-ACK.

The peon's body surged upright – pulled the fat guard forward a step. Some of the prisoners laughed – perhaps because the peon had reacted so much like someone who has their buttocks pinched when least expecting it. The guard leaned back on the rope, pulled the peon tight to the stake. There was no stripe on the peon's back. Some thought that Valdez had missed and the peon had jumped at the sound alone. Others, who could handle a bullwhip, knew that perhaps an inch of the tip had struck the peon with the force of a bullet.

Valdez, with a dour peasant's determination, settled to work. He set a rhythm that did not falter, and the crack of the lash was slow and constant. He started at the base of the spine and worked upwards. As he progressed, the lower cuts began to bleed. Soon the lower back of the peon was crimson. When the whip struck where it had struck before, blood splashed, and looping back it flicked red droplets over the crowd.

At first the guard had a tug-of-war on his hands, but the whip robbed the peon of strength. By the twenty-fifth stroke he was on his knees with his cheek flattened against the stake and with no strength to pull against the rope because all his strength was taken up by the shuddering of his limbs. It was not very long after going on his knees that he began to cry out.

Valdez reached the shoulder blades and began to work down again. The peon screamed under the lash and between strokes he sobbed and called on his patron San Antonio and on the Mother of God to rescue him.

The prisoners tried to show poker faces, but at each whiplash eyelids flickered, and here and there taut neck muscles would give a little spasm and a head would jerk. They watched and listened while the whip stole the peon's pride, then his self-respect, and then his reason.

Valdez coiled the whip. He walked over and stood before the peon. The peon knelt and sobbed. He never raised his eyes, but stared fearfully at Valdez's spread legs. And Valdez did not move. He looked ready to stand there till the sun sank behind the palms. At last the peon could stand it no longer. He went down and kissed Valdez's boot, leaving a smear on it from his bloody lips. There was laughter from the prisoners. When Valdez still did not move, the peon kissed the other boot.

Nullo had learned to read men across a poker table. His mind was as concentrated now as any time when his fortune hung on the flip of a card, and he had read the character of the peon in the first few minutes of his being dragged out. The peon had character and self-respect. His stubbornness had probably taken him through most of his twenties, but you could see he'd already lived long enough to learn to curse the spark of spirit that only made a peon's life bitter. Now he hated God for abandoning him and life for humbling him – and more than these he hated himself. The whip had hung over him all his life – and in a corner of his bitter heart he might have even longed for it.

'He better love his burro,' Valdez said. 'He will

never love a woman again.' The guards laughed. And there was laughter from the prisoners too, despite the fact that they did not like this flogging. The guards who had dragged him out now hauled the peon away.

The prisoners milled about, forming groups. Their laughter, loud talk and bluster told how their nerves were worked up. Nullo kept to the shade of the palm thatch and thought about the desert. To look at him it was hard to tell if his eyes were open, but he saw the knot of six men walking towards him.

Every village had a poster of Blanco, and his was not the sort of face to lose itself in the crowd. His hair and his albino skin were stark white in the noon glare. He was short, barrel-chested, with no neck and with legs half the length they should have been for his body. He walked as though he would walk through a brick wall if it were in the way. His eyes flickered this way and that and his fingers kept twitching.

He stopped three feet away, and stared at Nullo with his pink-rimmed albino eyes. He had the snout of a pig. When you looked him in the face you looked inside his nostrils. His hands had stopped twitching. He stood dead still.

Nullo leaned against the diagonal stud that braced the uprights of the kitchen. He met Blanco's eye, but without hostility.

Not good enough, Nullo thought. You could

show you weren't scared but it wasn't courage that Blanco respected.

Nullo took in the other five out of the corners of his eyes, and fixed on one. He was trying to look bad, but his eyes were apprehensive. His face was pleasant, with laughter lines around the eyes, and trying to look evil just made him look troubled.

Nullo allowed his lungs to fill and held his breath. He then reached into his back pocket. Blanco's eyes followed Nullo's movement. Nullo didn't hurry. His hand closed over the knife. He'd modified the knife. He'd opened and closed it a few thousand times, greased the point of swivel with sweat. Now the blade swung loose on the rivet.

Nullo stepped forward bringing the hand out of his back pocket. Because his movements were relaxed it did not seem so fast. But it happened in half a second. The hand came out, gave a twitch and the blade swung out and locked. The one with the laughter lines had just begun to realize he'd been chosen when the knife went in. Nullo stabbed him up under the chin. He pulled forward and up. He could feel the back of the chin-bone and the back of the teeth, could feel the underside of the tongue against the point of the blade. The man stood on tiptoes, his chin stretched forward. His eyes opened, rolled, fixed on Nullo's.

'Don't look at me with your fool's eyes.'

There were no guards around. No one could see

the knife. Only the men grouped around could see the blood trickling over Nullo's hand.

Blanco chuckled. 'It's true, he has a foolish face.'

Nullo slid out the knife and the man crouched with his hands to his neck. Drops of blood hit the dust in front of him. Nullo began to walk away.

'You have style, cowboy,' Blanco said.

He strode busily along beside Nullo. His men fell in on either side. Blanco turned and growled over his shoulder. One of his men shoved away the stabbed man, who was following, clutching his neck.

'Go to the infirmary, fool.'

'Say nothing, fool,' Blanco said. 'Change your foolish face before you show it to me again.'

It wasn't pleasant to walk beside Blanco. You could feel his glands pumping juice, feel his restless will working.

'Stop, cowboy.'

Nullo walked another couple of steps, then stopped and turned. Blanco stood dead still again, his eyes fixed on Nullo's, looking up from under. Nullo wondered what was coming. He thought Blanco probably wondered too.

'As soon as you said it I knew it was true. He is a fool. You are wise. Are you wise?'

'I'm not wise, Blanco, because I can't read and write.'

'You can't read or write? It doesn't matter.'

'Can you read and write?'

'Yes,' Blanco said. He shrugged. 'It doesn't matter.'

'Seems to me you're the wise one, Blanco.'

Blanco laughed. 'You're still smart. It is really nothing to read and write. Maybe I teach you some day.'

'It's a waste of time.'

Blanco clapped him on the back. 'Come on.'

It looked to Nullo like he'd found a new friend. Couldn't be helped.

Five

Except for a lovely jacaranda that shaded the old adobe cottage, Jaime Vargas's farm was not much to look at. Nevertheless, he felt his heart lift when it came in sight. He had walked for three days. Yesterday morning his sandals had given out. His feet bore up well, and if he kept walking they did not hurt, but if he stopped they let him know they had business to settle with him. Fear or some species of shyness had prevented him from changing any gold in the villages he had passed. A few wild nopales was all he had eaten, and cactus juice had slaked his thirst.

The corn was harvested, he saw. Carrying his broken sandals in his hand, he descended the hill, made his way through the sorghum and limped through the door of the sun-cracked adobe. He sat down at the table and listened to the buzz of flies and what his feet had to say. Through the back window he saw his wife. She was scowling. No one

40

could scowl like Maria, although when it came to scolding she lacked confidence and would become confused and say illogical things. She passed the window with a bundle of clothes in her arms. Her cheek was pinched and pale, he saw.

When she came through the door and saw him, she did not say a word. Whenever anything happened that roused her greatly, in her confusion she would try to pretend complete indifference. This habit exasperated Jaime, and out of stubbornness he kept silent.

But this was too much. She should at least say something. He looked out of the corner of his eye. Her face was not pale now. It was crimson. She laid the armful of dry clothes on the stool by the door and began folding them and placing the folded clothes on the one good chair they had. He thought she was shaking, he couldn't be sure. She was very brisk in her movements. There were two scowl lines above her nose, but with her face lit up the way it was the scowl was not effective.

She did not cry though. But his damned eyes were filling. And he did not even feel like crying. All he felt was his feet were throbbing so hard that he was surprised he could not see them expand and contract like a bullfrog's throat.

'I could eat some beans,' Jaime said.

She put a tin cup and a jug of pulque on the table. When she saw his eyes, her own eyes lit up like lamps. Jaime was displeased. Happy too.

Happy to see this light in her eyes, but displeased that it should be caused by the sight of his own wet eyes. Among the Mescalero it was very unusual to see anyone but children with tears in their eyes. Oh well, if it gave her pleasure.

He smiled. 'You see? I am not your husband, I am your sister.' He took her hand, and it was like touching a timorous rabbit. It was curious how easy it was to make her happy. 'The corn is harvested. So you have found another man?'

Maria burst out laughing. He had to wipe a little of her spittle from his face.

'Benito cut the corn,' she said. 'He is outside now.'

'Won't you bring him in and introduce him to your sister?'

'Yes, I shall tell him my baby sister is here.'

'I hope you do not mind that I smell.'

'No, I do not mind,' she said, hiding her face against his shirt, her voice trembling a little.

'Your family is well. . . ? And Lena. . . .'

'She is dead.'

'Oh.'

Jaime held her. Her back felt as narrow and fragile as any twelve-year-old girl's under her threadbare blouse.

'They think she ate something poisonous. She was vomiting and could not control her bowels.'

'Are you very unhappy?'

Lena was her sister. There had always been something wrong with her mind. She never

42

learned to speak. Sometimes they had to tie her
hands to stop her scratching and scratching at
her skin till the blood ran. Sometimes she would
sob for a day at a time, but mostly she smiled at
nothing. She had loved Maria more than anyone,
and Maria had always looked after her.

'I was. If not for something else, I would be very
unhappy. But . . . I believe that when God sends a
bad thing, if it is too much then He will also send
a good thing.'

'Yes, yes, there is a balance. God is very precise.'

'I am going to have a baby,' she whispered
against his shoulder. 'I did not even know, but the
old woman Oaxime told me. She is certain and she
is never wrong.'

'No. This is too much. Too much. I forbid you to
look at me.'

She turned obediently away. It was no good. He
walked briskly outside.

Why was he not made with a proper Indian's
stone face? Part of him was proud to be emotional
like a white man, but part of him distrusted it. He
wiped his eyes and thought: Well, today I will be a
white man. Poet and lover. It amuses Maria. He
went back inside, bowed low and humble like
love's slave.

'As men sift gold from earth, so God once
extracted the precious essence of all things lovely
to form a frowning angel that He named—'

The sound of a rough masculine cough brought

his head up with a jerk. Benito stood there, machete in hand, rubbing his neck with a rag, and the look he gave him verged on sour.

There, Jaime thought. See? Let that be a lesson to me. Oh well, I have no reputation anyway.

'Benito. Praise God for proper men. You have saved my corn and protected my wife. I will help you with your harvest though.'

'It is all in. How did you get out? Did you escape?'

'No, I will tell you all. Sit down and let us drink pulque.'

But Jaime did not tell Benito the whole truth. He was sorry not to take Benito into his confidence. But Benito was stolid and honest and he could not trust him to lie convincingly on his behalf. He told him he had bribed his way out of jail with gold. Gold that he had found on his land.

'Gold.' Benito scraped at the stubble of his chin.

'Gold.' Maria scowled. 'You did not tell me.'

'Must a husband tell his wife all his business? I was going to have a gold ring made and surprise you with it. Wait here.' Jaime got up. 'Hah, my feet. Wait here.' He went outside and, taking off his pants, removed the gold from the seam.

'There,' he said, laying the nuggets on the table. 'There.' He gave one to Benito. 'There will be more for you, but with this you can buy some coffee and bacon from the village. Gomez has scales in his store and he can weigh gold. And here,' he said to

Maria, 'this is for you. I want you to go into the village, buy yourself something nice and tell everyone what a generous husband you have. You too, Benito, tell them that Jaime Vargas is rich.'

'Is it wise?' said Benito.

'It cannot be a secret if I want to spend it. Let them know. They have despised me for my poverty long enough. Go now, Benito. Take Maria to the village with you. Let her buy brandy for us to celebrate my freedom and my fortune.'

'No time for brandy,' Benito said. 'The woman and the child are alone. It is not good to leave them long. Times are evil in this pig of a country.'

'But, Benito, go to the village first. Buy gifts for Rosaria and Carilda.'

With the idea of bacon and coffee in his mind, Benito was already half persuaded. Soon, accompanied by Maria, he started for the village.

And Jaime, while the sun crept towards the western sierras, sat with his back against the jacaranda and lent a sympathetic ear to the complaint of his feet.

Six

'Nullo. Nullo.'

Nullo looked down to see Porfirio hobbling by his elbow.

'I am – I – I – I am—'

'Your tongue limps too now.'

'I am worried.'

'Plenty to worry a man, cripple. Price of coffee's high.'

'I am very disturbed,' Porfirio whispered. He plucked at Nullo's sleeve, trying to draw him into the shadow of one of the arches that lined the south of the quadrangle.

'What is it?'

Three men were huddled behind the stone pillar. They stopped whispering and looked suspiciously at Nullo and Porfirio. One of them gave a jerk of the head and the other two followed him out into the glare of the yard. Porfirio watched them go, then whispered:

46

'Blanco has been speaking to me. He says he is going to break out. He asked me if I wanted to go with him.'

'Yeah, he asked me the same question.'

'What did you answer?'

'Why don't you ask him?'

'I don't want to go.'

'Then stay.'

'But I told him I would go.'

'Change your mind?'

'No. I couldn't tell him I did not want to go. I did not want to make him angry. When he asked me – he did not even ask me, it was one of his men, but he was watching me – I could not say no.'

'Why not?'

'Why not – are you crazy? With Blanco's eyes on me, for a start I am amazed that I could speak. I had an urge to shit in my pants. With his eyes on me, telling him no seemed as unthinkable as telling him his mother was a whore.'

'You're old and you're busted up. Why are you afraid for your worthless life?'

'I am old, my back is twisted, I have not two good teeth in my head. All is gone – youth, health, honour, pride. . . . All I have left is my fear. What reward is there for me in courage? Wait.' He clutched Nullo's sleeve. 'Please, I beg you to protect me.'

'Why do you think I'd help you?'

'You are . . . you are . . . good – no. . . .' Porfirio

47

searched Nullo's eyes, searched his own agitated mind. Confusion dulled his eyes and his scabbed mouth drooped open. 'These are all vicious animals – snakes and mad dogs. You . . . no, I do not know what species of animal you are. . . .'

'The world will get by without you, old man.'

'Yes,' Porfirio whispered, looking at his feet. A string of saliva began to droop from his lower lip. 'And you. . . ?'

But Nullo was already beyond earshot.

'Fresh *feesh*.'

Every ten minutes, Blanco's man would throw back his head and cry, 'Fresh *feesh*.' The third man they'd put in Nullo's cell was a fisherman from Colima, and Blanco's man Vicente, because he was nervous of Nullo, had begun to goad him.

'Fresh *feesh*.' Vicente let the cry ring out. He was very pleased to have invented this joke. Everyone who heard his 'Fresh fish' would know that he was not timid with the *Americano*. Blanco would hear him and know that Vicente was not a shy girl, but a man who was not afraid to make his voice heard.

Vicente wrinkled his nose and sniffed.

'Hey, Nullo, don't you smell a stink in here?'

'That's right, Vicente.' Nullo leaned with an elbow on the crossbar of the cell, thinking of the desert. He brought his mind back from the empty distances to the clammy hole of a cell and looked at the fisherman. 'A stink with scales on it.'

Vicente laughed with delight and said in the fisherman's pidgin dialect, 'Stink so much has scales on it. Why you fish no fresh, *cholo*?'

'You should see the tuna I catch one time past,' the fisherman said.

'Was it beautiful? Did you love it? Did you marry your tuna?'

Vicente roared with laughter and the fisherman lowered his eyes and tittered. Vicente turned to Nullo to see how he appreciated his joke. Nullo looked at him and saw Vicente's grin falter. He was about to drag up a laugh for the sake of harmony, when he felt something touch his leg.

He looked down and saw a hand poking through the bars of the cell. The cons often passed things from cell to cell. Sometimes the guards stopped them, but the Yaqui was on duty and he didn't let his shift interfere with siesta. The hand opened and Nullo bent and took a balled cigarette paper from the palm. A spent match had been used to write: 'Blanco wants the knife'.

Vicente craned over his shoulder. 'It starts,' he said.

'Looks like it.' Nullo took the knife out of his pocket.

'I thought you could not read?' Vicente said.

Nullo reached the knife through to the next cell.

Twenty minutes later, Blanco began shouting

49

for the guard. The Yaqui, his face puffed with sleep, passed their cell.

'What's the matter?' The Yaqui's voice was not steady.

'What's the matter?' they heard Blanco say. 'Are you blind? You see the blood that pours from his mouth and you ask what is the matter? He is vomiting blood. He has to go to the doctor at once. That is the matter, you piece of snipe from the nose of a pox-ridden whore.'

'Wait. I will bring Valdez and Ricardo.'

'Do you want him to die? He bleeds like a drunk pissing. Are you going to wake Valdez from his siesta? Are you going to wait while he drinks his afternoon coffee? This man is my dear friend.'

'You never met him before yesterday.'

'He is from the same village as I. If he dies, then I promise that you will die, crust from a shit-bucket. I will remove your ugly features one by one. I will stew your guts in a pan while your pig eyes watch.'

'I am not afraid of you, Blanco.'

The prisoners screeched at the wobble in the Yaqui's voice.

'Stand away from the bars,' The Yaqui commanded in a voice that was passably deep and authoritative, but with a note in it to let Blanco know that his position obliged him to speak like this. 'If you want me to help this piece of whore's filth then stand clear, or he can bleed till he drains.'

A key rattled.

'Oh,' they heard – a note of surprise that was followed by a gurgle. A high scream – also from the Yaqui – echoed along the corridor. It was suddenly cut short. There was another scream – this time from someone else.

'Blanco, *viva* Blanco,' Vicente yelled. 'Blanco, let me out.'

'In a minute. I have something I want to do.'

'But Blanco, hurry.'

'*Viva* Blanco,' the prisoners began yelling.

'Shut up,' Blanco shouted out. '*Madre di Dios*. There.'

Something hit the ground with a hollow 'bop'. One of the prisoners yelped. An eyeball rolled to a halt outside the cell.

Vicente howled with laughter. The fisherman began to moan.

'*Viva* Blanco.'

There was a shot. A moment later, Blanco appeared. He was soiled with blood like a butcher. He trod on the Yaqui's eye as he rammed the key home in the lock.

'The carcass of Ricardo is at the end of the hall,' Blanco told Vicente. 'Go and get his key and gun.'

They heard shouting from the direction of the western cellblock. Shots were fired, and the voice of Valdez roared commands. No guards appeared in their block however. The cells emptied and the corridor filled with yelling prisoners.

Blanco's voice rapped out:

'Quiet. . . . Those that said they did not want to come with me – into this cell . . . where you will be safe.' Blanco rattled the barrel of the Yaqui's Colt against the bars of cell in which the Yaqui's headless corpse lay beside one of Blanco's cell mates, who bled from the mouth and the belly. Blanco's pink-rimmed eyes burned with confident energy.

'I've changed my mind. I want to come with you.' It was the fisherman.

'Too late.'

Blanco pushed him into the cell. Six others entered the cell – walked in on their own, or were shoved in.

'I feel I made a right decision.'

Nullo found Porfirio at his elbow.

'Something tells me you did.'

'Thank God for my coward's heart.'

'Please, let me come with you, Blanco,' a man in the cell said.

'You have two weeks of your term to serve. Why break out?'

'Please.' The man reached his hand through the bars.

Blanco snarled and rapped the hand with the Colt's barrel.

'Listen,' he told the men in the cell. 'You have all heard stories about me. They say I lust for the screams of men. They call me monster. They say I am mad for blood.' Blanco laughed, and some of the men in the cell answered with their own shaky laughter. 'Well, all this is quite true,' Blanco said. 'But I put you a fair question, whether you wanted to escape or not, and you answered fairly. So I will be fair with you. You can take the chance that our breakout will not succeed – that we will all be captured and locked up again – or . . . you can kill yourselves.'

The fisherman giggled.

'Kill ourselves?'

Blanco nodded.

'But . . . how?' someone asked timidly.

Blanco frowned. 'Well, if you want me to do it for you I will. But you know how it is with me: with women I am slow and patient because I love to hear their sounds of pleasure, while with men I am also very slow because the sound of pleasure is pale and weak compared to the sincere expression of agony. I am not evil. I think I am a little crazy, but I am not evil. No, I am just truthful to nature. We will leave you now, but when it is over we will return – in victory, or defeat, who knows?'

Blanco made a signal to Vicente and Nullo and one of his other men and began to push through the crowd of prisoners.

'How will we kill ourselves?' a voice pleaded. 'How without weapons?'

Blanco was not much of a strategist, but he was brave. A knot of guards milled before the door of the western block. Blanco, with the Yaqui's pistol in one hand and Ricardo's in the other, charged across the yard straight for them. Valdez turned and levelled his revolver. The phlegmatic peasant's lantern jaw was set firmly, and he did not allow Blanco's blazing pistols to hurry his aim. A .45 slug punched through his cheek and ricocheted around inside his skull. His brains scrambled, Valdez dropped. Another of Blanco's bullets somehow found a mark. A second guard went down. On hands and knees he poured a stream of blood from his stomach on to the dust like water from a tap. By now the rest of the guards had bolted into the block and shut the door.

The governor, half-way across the yard, turned and fled for the shelter of his quarters. A wave of convicts flowed across the quadrangle. Like a man with the flood at his heels who scrambles for higher ground, the governor dashed up the steps that led to his quarters. But the sea of convicts engulfed him, and he was dragged back down the steps, boot heels foremost.

When they stood him before Blanco, with his great flowing moustaches he looked like a crestfallen walrus – one that seeks with its eyes to make you understand that, though it has made mistakes, at heart it is not an evil walrus.

Blobs of revolting spittle splattered against the governor's face and his head rocked under blows and cuffs; and these he accepted without resentment, but only seeming to beg humbly, silently, for a little sympathetic understanding.

Blanco began laying about him.

'Leave him alone, you dogs. Look at them,' he said to the governor, gazing round him with disgust.

The governor nodded, tried to smile. Blanco crunched his nose with a punch.

'Look at them, I said.'

Snuffling blood, the governor hastily turned, glanced furtively from one to another of the faces.

'Are they not dogs?'

The governor mumbled something.

'What?'

'I – you see – no.'

'You contradict me?'

'Yes,' the governor said hastily.

'You do?'

'No. It was yes to your . . . your other . . .'

'You call me dog?' Porfirio demanded, limping up to the governor. There was a crazed merriment in his eyes. 'I will pull off your whiskers.'

The governor yelped as Porfirio began hauling at his moustache. Blanco lost interest in the governor and strode over to the western block. He put his hands to his mouth and called out:

'Are we safe, Gomez?'

A voice shouted back from inside the cellblock:

'You are safe if you stay to the side of the block. They cannot aim a gun through these holes.'

The little window holes just under the roof tiles were less than six inches square on the outside.

There was a door and a gate at either end of the block.

'Call on your men to surrender,' Blanco ordered.

The governor did as he was bid, but his men did not. Blanco beckoned the governor to him and said:

'If you can make them come out, I will let you go.'

Not one of those who were close enough to hear believed Blanco. If the governor were a bystander he would not have believed either, but in the circumstances his terror made him credulous.

A leather armchair was carried out on to the veranda of the governor's quarters, and Blanco sat in it and watched the governor sweat in the sun as he pleaded and cajoled, made outrageous promises, threatened and even wept in his efforts to make the guards surrender.

Seven

The guards did not intend trusting to the mercy of Blanco and the convicts. Blanco just wanted his three men – and particularly Gomez, whose shrewd brain he relied on – released from the western block. The guards agreed to this, but the other prisoners wanted to liberate their comrades. The guards, however, feared that with only themselves in the block the prisoners would smoke them out. In the end, Blanco's three men were let out, and the prisoners grew bored with the siege and with their sentiments of solidarity.

'Those others, have they succeeded in killing themselves?'

'One of them was successful only in rendering himself unconscious,' Gomez told Blanco.

The governor was becoming very uneasy about Blanco's promise to set him free. Plucking up courage, the man approached Blanco and began to whisper humbly and earnestly to him. At last

Blanco made a gesture and, with the governor trotting before, they disappeared into the governor's quarters. Some minutes later, they reappeared on the veranda. Blanco called Gomez and Vicente, who went in and dragged out a woman of around thirty-five and an adolescent boy. The governor essayed a protest, but Blanco, suddenly impatient, turned him about by his collar and delivered a kick to the seat of the pants that sent him tottering down the steps of the veranda.

Blanco found a machete in the kitchen. He formed the prisoners into a circle in the yard. The governor and the man who had failed to despatch himself were pushed into the middle of it. Blanco, machete in hand, entered the circle and put on a display.

Nullo watched. He felt many of the emotions and sensations that most of the others felt at the spectacle, but part of his mind was on the desert. He thought of the dry heat and empty silence. He had a notion to go there, just why he did not know, but he thought if he spent some time there maybe he could work out his next move.

After an hour, Blanco's two victims – still alive but unable to respond satisfactorily – were left to the flies. Blanco had wearied himself chasing them about the circle of prisoners. He called for a bottle of wine, which he tipped to his lips and kept there till he'd drained it. His animal energy – the secret of his dominance – did not fail him long.

Soon, restored, he took the governor's wife – who had not ceased screaming for the last hour – and when he was finished with her he threw her to the prisoners. The governor's son, however, he did not lay a finger on.

The men grew weary. It was the hour when the mosquitoes rose from the mangrove swamps. The cicadas grew more shrill and grating. Nullo looked at the sky. Above the palms it was purple and yellow like bruised skin. In an hour the moon would be up, and nobody showed any sign of stirring out of here. When it got full dark he should make a move. Though he didn't know what to do for the best. He knew nothing about the country, and he didn't like the thought of going alone through the jungle without a gun, not if it was true about Indians patrolling it who brought back runaways' heads for a bounty. When it was dark he would see how he felt. Meantime, he made his way through the knots of men to the pump. There was a dry skin on his lips, and right down his throat to his belly he was husk dry.

'Are you wondering why I did not harm the boy?'

Nullo straightened up from the water pump. Blanco stood there, squat and powerful, his shirt and pants stiff with gore.

'I guess you got your reasons,' Nullo said.

'You are right. This reason: those that you kill cannot hate you. So, I always leave one alive.

Think of this: right at this moment, from Durango to Vera Cruz, there are twenty, perhaps thirty, people thinking about me right now ... and hating me. . . . You, come here.'

Porfirio limped forward. He grinned impudently and tried not to tremble.

'Do you want to come with me to the mountains?'

Porfirio did not, but it was not easy to say no to Blanco, so he tried to look honoured and said, 'Yes, Excellency.'

'Well then, you can, if you answer me a question. Is it better to be loved or hated?'

'I am not the sort of man who is either loved or hated.'

'No, you ghost,' Blanco said. 'You are a matter of indifference among men. I shall tell you: to be loved is to be despised – a little. But to be neither loved nor hated is to be ignored. Can I be ignored?'

'Never, Excellency.'

'I will ask you another question.'

'My wits are feeble, Excellency.'

'Does fear beget love or does it beget hate?'

'I do not know, Excellency. I am a dung beetle, and all my study is dung. I know nothing else.'

'Shall I tell you the secret of success, Nullo? With fear there is respect. If they fear you enough they will even love you – and yet respect you too. You do not fear me, Nullo.'

'I'm afraid of you, Blanco.'

Perhaps with Blanco it was better to show some fear. But generally it was as dangerous to show fear as courage.

'You can come with me, Nullo.'

'Thanks.' The old man had said it: it was hard to say no to Blanco. Nullo wondered what stopped Blanco from starting trouble with him now, just to show who was boss.

'I will only take as many as there are horses in the stable. Which are twelve. This old ghost I take because it is good for a gang to have someone that everyone can be boss of. But you, Nullo, you could be my lieutenant . . . perhaps. Would you like to ride with me and be my lieutenant, Nullo?'

'As long as you can promise me some fun. When I get out of here I want to raise some hell. Make up for the time I spent cooling my heels in this shit-hole.'

Blanco came close and Nullo was enveloped in the choking odour of blood. Blanco had the look of a man who's caught the ring of a false note.

'You want to drink, whore, spill blood, is that right?'

'That's about right.'

'There is an agent of the American government hunting me. His name is Ransome. Is your name Ransome?'

'I don't guess so.'

'The American government is not pleased with me. The reason they are not pleased is because I

61

raided the camp of the Pacific Mining Company. I killed everyone, including the six American employees of the company, and two officers of the American Navy – engineers sent to install a hydraulic engine for the company. But maybe you know all this?'

'First I heard, Blanco. American government's got no more time for me than it has for you. That's what brings me south of the big river. Hotter'n Satan's asshole up there for me.'

'What's your racket, my friend Nullo?'

'I'm a gambler.'

'What do you think of me, Nullo? Some think I am a monster.'

'I got nothing against you.' This was true. And the word monster did not mean anything to Nullo.

'Good,' Blanco said. He threw his arms wide and shouted, 'Good for you, my friend the gringo.' Then: 'We are going to need money for our drinking and whoring.'

From his pocket he brought something wrapped in a white handkerchief. He opened the handkerchief in the cup of his palm, held it so that only he could see inside.

'I know where we can find money. Plenty too. They say fortune smiles on the brave. I say fortune is a fat whore, Nullo, and it's time I put her on her back again.'

Eight

Blanco and his men rode out of the gate in the midst of an army of prisoners. The horses picked up speed and the men on foot gave way before them, watching dumb-eyed as they trotted by. Some kept pace running. Afraid to say anything to Blanco, they dropped behind one by one.

They left the road and came to a river. The tropical moon shone on the backs of caymans cooling themselves in the bank's slime. Those with weapons levelled them on the 'gators. Nullo had only the knife. Blanco had let him have it back, but the five pistols and the two rifles he kept among his own men. On the far bank of the river they made a camp and the men started drinking. Nullo drank a little for the sake of appearances.

Gunfire, far to the south, made the camp fall silent. There was a garrison of *federales* half-way between the prison and the town of San Cristobal. They might have got word of the escape or else a patrol had chanced upon the prisoners. After the gunfire stopped the men kept a silent camp for ten or fifteen minutes, but it was soon rowdy as before.

Nullo didn't think if he could help it and never made plans. Now, whatever instinct it was that told him to rest or stay was beginning to stir. He was like a salted worm. The sweaty heat of the night and the mosquitoes whining at his ear irked him. The never-ending jeering and boasting, the screech of drunken laughter that Porfirio used like a scared dog uses its bark, all grated on his nerves. And for appearances' sake, whether he liked it or not, he had to add his own voice to it. So he picked on Vicente. A *charro* had stolen Vicente's woman and Nullo picked on that. Vicente laughed and hid his feelings well, but he didn't make any comeback, and Nullo could feel the others' respect for himself grow. But Blanco poked some fun at Nullo's Spanish. It wasn't much – Blanco knew he wasn't to be treated too lightly – still Nullo could tell that Blanco could do to him what he'd done to Vicente if he wanted. He knew they would all get behind Blanco if he started. He felt vulnerable now, a foreigner and unarmed. Give him a gun in each hand, he thought, and he could blast them all to hell just for a little silence.

Not that there'd be any silence in this hothouse. The jungle was a slut that bred easy and from the ceibas and mangroves its brood sang the song of the tropics. The cicadas took the treble and the frogs in the bulrushes kept a bass that jarred like the rasp of hell's hinges.

Nullo took it easy on the wine and tried to work out a gambler's odds against making a break or staying. The odds were for staying now, but the longer he stayed the worse they would become. Vicente, scared by Nullo's attack, had tried to ingratiate himself. He sat back against the same ceiba and now, full of wine and brandy, his head lolled on his chest. Nullo's eyes strayed to the butt of the Colt holstered at his side. It was a good moment to make a break. He felt it was only a matter of time before they turned on him. If he believed in omens, the butt of the Colt just to his hand seemed like a good one.

What gambler didn't believe in omens? If he walked up to Blanco and put a bullet in his brain, he might just take the fight out of the others. That's what he felt like doing. But it was stupid. Just edginess talking. If he was going to go, he should go quiet, when everyone was asleep.

Nullo slipped the gun out of the holster. He broke out the magazine, clicked it back in place and slid the Colt back where it came from. If you were going to believe in omens, an empty gun seemed a plain enough one. Nullo lay back against the tree and willed his nerves to relax.

Next day, when they'd put the *federales'* garrison behind them they climbed well out of the mangroves and headed for high country. Blanco seemed to know where he was going. He had the look of a man who has a plan. Gomez probably knew what it was. Maybe Vicente did too. But Blanco didn't like to let the rest of them feel over-important by letting them in on too much. They rode through prickly pear and agave and then through cultivated land. Blanco steered clear of the farmhouses and shacks that began to appear. But on the third day as the dust-reddened sun sank low they came to a farm that clung to the poor dirt of a terrace on the foothills of the sierras. The farmer, gleaning a cornfield; looked up from his work as he saw them head for his house. They dismounted outside the shack and waited for the farmer.

'Is your name Vargas?' Blanco asked him.

The farmer was about thirty-five, grey-haired, used up with labour. His face was not of the expressive kind, but there was a glitter of apprehension in his eye.

'No,' the farmer answered.

'What is your name?'

'Benito Dias.'

The door of the shack opened and a woman looked out. She drew a shawl over her head and clutched it to her neck.

'Good day, *señora*,' Blanco said.

A young girl with a freckled face appeared

behind the woman and gazed at Blanco with wide eyes.

'Where is the home of this Vargas?' Blanco asked.

'I do not know any Vargas,' said the farmer.

'You admire my fair skin?' Blanco asked the girl.

The girl gazed at Blanco, tense-faced, but too innocent to suspect trouble. There was a slight turn in one of her eyes.

The woman made to push the girl back inside.

'Woman, bring out your daughter.'

The woman's eyes went from her husband to Blanco. She bowed her head, laid it a little to the side and gave a piteous glance around the men, not raising her eyes higher than their chests. She looked like a baby that's about to stick out its lower lip and sob. Making the sign of the cross, she murmured:

'El Blanco.'

Blanco's white eyebrows came together in a deep frown and he put a hand on the machete in his waist-sash. Slowly – with a touch of burlesque in the movement – he began to draw the machete.

The woman and the girl stared at him like mesmerized rabbits. Blanco slowly drew the machete, keeping his eyes fixed on them all the time, then, when it was almost out of the sash, he stopped. He goggled, grimaced, and gave a theatrical growl.

The child giggled.

The woman gave him a look. The most accomplished actress might have tried in vain to recreate that expression – a play of emotions, with barely a movement of the features, in which fear became relief, then reproach, and . . . the beginning of love.

Blanco beckoned the girl. She gave a shake of her head, smiling. Blanco hunched his shoulders and hung his head and looked dejected. He beckoned again, and the girl, with a giggle, came to him. Blanco patted her short brown hair.

Nullo was struck by Blanco's face. It was strange to see that tender expression on it. And he looked a little tired. That sat oddly on him too. It was Blanco's energy that drew men to follow him. With Blanco there was the promise of unflagging excitement. He joked and needled, told stories, laughed or raged – but he always kept your pulse beating fast.

'Aye me,' Blanco sighed. 'I could drink some wine. Do you have wine?'

'We have pulque – wait.' The woman disappeared.

A small mongrel came running round the corner of the shack. It began to bark as soon as it saw the men. It was a spirited dog and it ran up to Blanco and began to bark heatedly at him.

The evening was mild and calm, with the low sun mellow on the dusty yard and the rough pine boards of the shack, but there was something very jarring about the aggressive yapping of this mongrel. Blanco began to look irritated.

The dog made a little dart at Blanco and Blanco raised the machete. In a flash, he mongrel had turned and scampered out of reach. Then it began to turn to renew the skirmish. It made a half turn before it realized that it was not out of range after all. Blanco took another step forward and clove it where its hindquarters joined its spine. The dog lay in the dust motionless, unable to bark now, able to move nothing now but its eyes. Its spine was severed and its haunches were almost apart from its body.

Crockery smashed. The woman stood in the doorway with a broken jug at her feet. Her lips quivered and a piercing scream made the horses grunt and stamp.

Blanco stared at the woman. His face slowly contorted. His eyes were fixed on the woman but they saw nothing. This rage had nothing to do with her. It had been there, like fever sleeping in the liver, and whatever had woken it did not matter now it was building. When his veins were gorged and his whole being was congested with rage he put back his head and screamed at the red-barred sky.

'I am Blanco and I drink blood. I will stew in the pit of hell, you sluts and whores and bastards. You will be happy when you see that. Scream, you whore. Blanco shall roast till his eyeballs pop. Weep, you whore.'

Porfirio gave a screech of laughter. Blanco turned on him and Porfirio clapped his hands to his mouth and shook his head. Blanco bit his hand and made to rush the men. They gave ground, laughing at themselves for flinching, and then yelling too, with their eyes hot with Blanco's fever. Blanco ground words of rage and hate from his congested throat and with every word their eyes burned hotter. The priests and politicians and lawmakers had words, but Blanco showed them they had their own words too. Those others were all false and their words were lies, only fit for women, who fed on lies. Blanco gave them hard, strong words. But they knew in their hearts they did not need words. The truth lived in the blood and it was known to men before the first word was ever spoken. And Blanco did not use words like coward to justify himself, he used them now to work himself up. He was ready now and he took a handful of the woman's hair.

'Leave her alone.'

Benito's hand was on the cutlass at his side, but his face showed that he would not use it.

Blanco turned and gazed at Benito. Surprise seemed to have made him forget his rage.

'Leave them alone? What sort of men do you think we are?' As he spoke, the tone of surprise faded, and word by word the great rage grew and choked his voice. 'We do not leave women alone. It is for a ghost of a man like you to leave women alone. Your lust is gone and women do not fear you, because you are like a woman yourself. Do you smile and coo and pat her little hand? I will show you what a man does with a woman.'

Nullo watched what followed with the females and knew it was dangerous not to join in. When Toto grabbed the girl, Nullo took a handful of his hair and pulled him off.

'My turn,' he shouted and hit Toto. Toto did not offer to fight, but Nullo kept hitting him. Already Porfirio had hold of the howling girl and the men were laughing and egging him on. Nullo hoped that they'd think he and Toto were fighting, but really he was just beating Toto. He grappled with Toto and at last Toto began to show some resistance.

'I'll kill you,' he whispered to Toto and saw the fear in his eyes.

He released his grip a little. Enough for Toto to pull free. He went for Toto and Toto began to run. Nullo managed it so that he steered him into the corn. Hidden by the corn, he caught up with Toto and knocked him cold with a rock. Nullo crept back through the cornstalks. When he got to the end of the field he knelt and watched through the dry brown leaves. Vicente fired the shack and as it blazed Blanco began to kill the females. Nullo knelt and watched. The farmer, tied by the clothes line to the clothes-post, did not watch but had to listen to the screaming. At last it was over. Blanco stood up and turned to face the setting sun and threw something from him. It was the girl's arm. Nullo crept back, hoisted Toto on to his back and carried him out of the corn.

'This bastard made me miss all the fun,' he said, dumping Toto on the ground. Blanco turned his blood-spotted face and gave him a level look.

Nullo knew he'd made a mistake. He should have joined in with them. What would it have mattered to those two females? He didn't pretend he felt anything for them. Pity is a trick the weak try to play on you. But when someone suffers like those two, you don't feel pity, just revulsion.

'The fun is not over, Nullo the gringo. The farmer told me what I wanted to know, and we are going to ride and soon there will be more fun.'

'Kill me,' the farmer pleaded.

'Kill yourself, if you have the guts,' Blanco said as he mounted.

'Freedom,' Porfirio cried in an ecstasy.

The men laughed and Blanco too turned in his saddle with a smile on his face.

'Freedom. I never knew what it meant before. My mind is a sword and it slices rock. *Viva* Blanco.'

Nine

Blanco reined his horse, motioned the others on, and waited till Nullo drew level. 'This man Ransome, they say he is very good with a gun.'

Nullo was thinking that he should have made a break that first night in the mangroves, gun or no gun. There was no wine or brandy to put them in a stupor now, and Blanco had taken a notion to be a proper commander and set two armed men on look-out every night. He'd given up lying awake waiting for a chance. He needed to be rested and alert, because if he showed weakness they would turn on him. There was plenty of camaraderie among them, but they feared each other too. In a situation like that men looked for a scapegoat.

'Are you good with a gun, Nullo?'

'I'm from Texas.'

'I believe this man Ransome is a Texan too. They say he has killed some men. Have you ever killed anyone, Nullo?'

'I saw some fighting in the army.'

'So, you were a Yankee dogface?' Blanco sang:
' "And on her knee she wore a yellow garter. She wore it for her lover in the US Cavalry. CAVAL-REEE". Did some little Yankee girl wear your yellow garter, Nullo?'

'That's for officers. Dogfaces don't give girls garters and such. More like to give them the pox.'

'Ha, ha. I like you, Nullo. I would like to make you my friend. It's a long time since I had a friend. I am like the dog that is bitten and becomes shy. Have you heard this proverb, Nullo?'

'I heard it.'

'It is hard to find a true friend in this world. People betray you. Once I had a friend who betrayed me. It was very painful. Of course, I suppose it was more painful for this other – this false friend. He made plenty of noise when I used that steel brush – you know the kind of brush a plumber uses to polish pipe?'

Blanco gave a sidelong glance from his pink-rimmed eyes.

Nullo wondered if Blanco would like him to start trembling. Maybe. But it was as dangerous to show cowardice as courage. It might take the pressure off if he showed Blanco some fear. But then, Blanco might push it too far. He knew from experience there was a limit to what he could take. That kind of pride could get you into trouble, but in the long run more people backed off from it than tried to challenge it.

'Do you know what really hurt, Nullo?'

'Well, I guess you must have felt kind of let down.'

'I do not mean me. I mean this fart from a carcass that was my friend. What really hurt was the sulphur I rubbed in after.'

They came to a wheel-rut track that skirted a field of sorghum and led to an adobe farmhouse that slept in the shade of a flowering jacaranda.

Entering the adobe, they found a peasant in a ragged smock sitting at his kitchen table being served a bowl of hominy soup by a pretty Indian girl.

Jaime Vargas's eyes rested on Nullo for a moment longer than on the rest, but he gave no other sign of recognition.

'Forgive the intrusion,' Blanco said. He took off his sombrero and hung it from the corner of the door.

Jaime carefully replaced the wooden spoon in his bowl of soup and produced a quite convincing smile. 'You are forgiven.'

Blanco's looked at Jaime, looked at the girl. He found his groin suddenly itchy and gave it a scratch.

'Ah, piss on your forgiveness. Do you know who I am?'

'You are my brother in the eyes of God, and I think you are hungry. Please, will you share my food?'

'What is to drink?'

'We have some pulque. Maria. Serve the *caballeros*.'

Blanco was silent and no one else spoke until the girl served as many of them as she had cups for. The girl suffered under their eyes, and the colour in her cheeks and the quiver of her eyelid only made her more desirable. Blanco murmured:

'A little dove, this *chiquita*.' To Jaime Vargas he said, 'Thank you, thank you. Do I have the honour of addressing Señor Vargas?'

'Vargas? You are looking for Jaime Vargas? But why do you want him? He is a little person of no consequence. However, if you seek him' – Jaime pointed through the back window – 'continue on for half a day across the valley and you will come to his farm.'

'This is Vargas. This here is Jaime Vargas, Excellency,' Porfirio pushed his way through the men crowding the kitchen. 'He was in the prison. Before you came. He shared a cell with Nullo.'

Blanco looked sharply at Nullo.

'You know each other?'

'We shared a cell.'

'Yes, it is true. I shared a cell with this gringo. And greetings to you, my dear friend Porfirio. I did not see you among the company. How I have missed you. He snores like a pig, the gringo, you know. I do not miss him at all.'

'If you know him, he knows your name, so why

did you try to lie in front of him?'

'I lie? I joke merely. I joke all the time.'

'I am not laughing.'

'My jokes are rarely successful. I should give them up and try to win respect as a serious person.'

'You should give your mouth a rest, you pimple on a man's ass.'

The girl gave a gasp and turned to see who had prodded her. Vicente stood grinning with his Colt in his hand. Now that she faced him, he prodded between her legs with the barrel. She drew back, crimson-faced and scowling.

'El Blanco, please do not harm my wife,' Jaime said. 'I beg you. I am a poor man that even God despises. I have nothing. Nothing but what you see. If you see anything fit for taking, please take it and leave us in our misery. You are a great leader and fighter. I am just a worm. Not even worth the soiling of your boot to crush me.'

'It is not true, my friend. You are a man of consequence. You are a rich man. You have gold.'

'Gold? Ha, ha. No, no – ah, but I see. It's a lie. A lie I told for my own purposes – stop – leave her alone.'

Blanco turned and with a flick of the arm sent a stream of pulque into Vicente's face.

'Can you think of nothing but whores? Let her be so that I may have the attention of this peasant.'

'*Dios*. It stings.' Vicente dropped the Colt on the table the better to use both hands to rub his eyes.

'And you,' Blanco turned back to Jaime, 'why are you so concerned about the bitch. Is she your wife?'

'Yes, Excellency.'

'So much the worse. How is it – do you have to pretend you love her before she will let you on top? Or perhaps you do think you love her. Perhaps you are one of these miserable half-men-half-curs that women lead on a leash. Do you tell yourself you are in love because it is easier than facing the truth of your spineless lack of independence? Well, my Romeo, tell me where you have hidden your gold or I will cut off the nose of your Juliet.'

'Excellency, I swear by my mother I have no gold. Let me ex—'

'No gold?'

Blanco reached in his pocket and brought out a bunched handkerchief.

'What is this?'

He spilled Nullo's gold on to the table.

'He has no gold,' Nullo said. 'That's mine. I gave it to him so he could bribe his way out of prison.'

Blanco scratched his head. 'Ah, yes, yes, it is quite clear. Crystal clear. It is as clear as a cursed whore's piss.'

'If you don't believe me, ask Porfirio.'

'I know nothing of this,' Porfirio said with unac-

78

customed firmness. 'I am not involved. Do not let this man – this gringo – drag me into it. Besides . . . I need to crap.'

Saying this, Porfirio pushed past Nullo and shot through the door. Nullo let him go. It didn't make any difference. Gold or no gold, there was going to be bloodshed.

'I think you are false, gringo,' Blanco said. 'I want to find out your name too. But that can wait till later. In the meantime, I will use your knife to cut off the nose of the bitch. Have you anything to tell me before the bleeding starts, Romeo?'

'I beg you to listen. I tell you there is no—'

'No, don't tell me that. Gringo, your blade.' Blanco held out his hand without turning his head.

When Blanco gave an impatient snap of the fingers, Nullo reached back and eased his hand into his hip pocket. His thumb traced the knurls of the knife's bone handle. He drew it out. With a twitch of the wrist the blade swung out and locked. Jaime Vargas looked at the blade, then his eyes flicked up and fixed on Nullo's. Blanco's eyes narrowed. His hand edged towards the gun at his side. Without taking his eyes off Nullo, he said quietly:

'Tell me where the gold is, or my friend Nullo will begin on the face of your pretty wife.'

Staring into Nullo's eyes, Jaime Vargas said:

'You must do what you must, Excellency. It

would grieve me very much to see my wife hurt,
but if I have no gold I cannot prevent it.'

Blanco made a sudden fierce turn. Outside the
window-screen a woodchuck called, and three
shrill notes pierced the silence of the kitchen. A
fly buzzed briefly. Blanco said:

'I could cut her into fish-bait, couldn't I? Then I
would have to believe that there truly is no gold.
Otherwise, surely you would have said a word to
save your Juliet. Ah, but the world is full of
Juliets for a Romeo who has gold. Except . . . what
use is gold to Romeo if he has no *cojones*?' Blanco
brought up his hand with the first two fingers and
thumb extended. 'Do you see these fingers? I am
going to use them to crush your right testicle. And
then – not before – I will give you a chance to
talk.' Jaime's stool rasped on the floor. Gomez
pushed Jaime back down on the stool as Blanco's
hand reached for his groin.

Nullo caught a movement from the girl. For an
instant he thought she'd swooned and was
collapsing. Blanco must have noticed something
from the corner of his eye too. He turned and
stared into the barrel of Vicente's Colt that the
girl had snatched off the table. It trembled in her
hand as she heaved back on the hammer.

Nullo slung the knife.

The Colt clattered on to the table, and the girl's
hands went to the bone handle sticking from her
breast. Nullo crossed the room in two swift steps.

He went down on his knee and gripped the knife-handle. She was still alive. Drawing the knife, he gave it a twist. The shock finished her.

A shove sent him sprawling. He rolled and came up on his knee ready to grapple with Jaime Vargas.

But nothing existed for Jaime except his dead wife. He hunched over her, gazed into her fixed eyes. When he raised his head, tears were spilling over his cheeks. His eyes found Nullo's. A tear dropped from his chin on to his wife's face. He sniffed, and becoming aware of his tears, wiped a hand over his cheeks.

'Don't mind these,' Jaime said and made an effort to keep his face from crumpling.

Nullo stared back at him without expression.

'Don't mind these, you miserable bastard. I always cried too easily.'

Blanco stepped across to Nullo and put out his hand. Nullo took it and pulled himself up.

'You saved my life.'

'Do you think I would let her get a loaded gun?' Vicente said.

'It was not loaded? But Nullo did not know that, did you?'

'No.'

Blanco looked like a man who's bitten on something strange, who doesn't know if he should swallow or spit.

'So, it is true there is no gold?' he said at last.

'No more than what's on the table.'

'No gold?' Blanco repeated – but absently. The question that was on his mind went unasked. 'Well . . . the world is full of money. Let us seek it, eh?'

'What about him?' Vicente said.

Blanco kept looking at Nullo while the unframed question struggled in his albino eyes. 'Eh?' He turned, glanced at Jaime Vargas. 'We shall let him live, Nullo. His hate will be worth something to you. The man is nothing who is not hated.' Blanco plucked his sombrero off the door. He stood and looked at the hat for several seconds. Then, suddenly aware of all their eyes on him, he said:

'Burn the hovel and let us go.'

Ten

'Why did you do that?'

Blanco spoke in a whisper, but it carried easily to Nullo who rode just behind. No birds sang amongst the withered vegetation. In the windless silence the chink of spurs, the creak of saddles and the breathing of horses were loud. From time to time a pebble dislodged by a hoof clattered echoing down the slope to where far below hidden under dry brown scrub a river ran with a faint sigh. Blanco edged his horse to the side of the path to let Nullo draw level.

'Eh, why did you do what you did last night?' That look, the question that had clouded his eye as Jaime Vargas wept over the corpse of his wife, was there once more. He spoke in a whisper so the others, strung out along the path, should not hear.

'You're talking about the girl?'

'Why did you save my life?'

'There were no bullets in that gun, remember?'

Blanco nodded. Without turning his head he watched Nullo. Nullo kept a poker face and waited.

'You have the gift of *machismo*,' Blanco whispered. In the gloom, his white skin showed ghostly against the motionless fronds and drooping palm leaves. 'It is a rare thing, *machismo*.' He gave a slight motion of the head to indicate the others riding behind. 'Oh, these think they have it. They can be courageous when their blood is hot. But when it's cool they live in fear.'

Blanco raised a huge, decay-mottled leaf out of Nullo's path. 'To be unafraid in the quiet of your heart, that is noble. True *machismo* is nobility of spirit. You have it, and I recognize it because I too possess it. You look at me?'

'Not at you.' Nullo was looking at where the rocks, rising out of the gloom of the valley, were reddened by the setting sun. Blanco glanced up there – for an instant – then turned back, said:

'Can a man soaked in the blood of women and children have nobility of spirit? What do you see?'

'Nothing. Nothing now.' Through the gap in his teeth he sent a bead of spit between the horse's ears.

'It is a question of the degree of the crime. There is no nobility in thieving a loaf of bread. But great evil . . . that demands a great spirit. In Heaven the Devil was a very splendid fellow – so the scripture tells us. I care less for what my finger finds in my nostril than I do for the judgement of priests and old women. But when a man finds his equal, then he may consider his opinion. What do you think of me, Nullo?'

'I think you want to die,' Nullo whispered and kept his eye on the rocks. 'Why else would you let people live who hate you?'

'I don't know about dying. What I would like with all my heart is to sleep for a month.'

'No rest for you, Blanco.'

'Yes, you understand. No rest. No rest for Blanco. I could not have lived as one of the herd. Every atom of my being strove for fame. The energy it took – enough to heave the wheel of one of your Mississippi paddleboats – if they could have made steam from it. But when the prize is won . . . there is no rest. The pack leader cannot weaken or the pack will turn on him. Perhaps one like me should die young, in the fullness of power. But do I want to die? A mason who spends twenty years laying brick on brick, does the desire for death creep into his heart – or does he only want a change? There is someone up in those rocks.'

'Could be a prospector.'

'Could be *federales*.'

'Could be. They got us boxed, if it is.'

The jungle to their right started high now. They would have to climb into it, pull themselves up into it by their arms, even if they could get through the tangle. The slope to the river was steep and bare before it reached the vegetation that hid the river except for one scrub-covered outcrop.

'There's cover under that ceiba scrub. But it's as dangerous to break off and head for it as it is to keep going.'

'Twenty years I have been a bandit. That is what I wanted to be. A child can play at being a bandit, and the next day he can be something else . . . ah, this life of mine. . . .'

Blanco halted and dismounted. The strung-out men caught up and bunched around him.

'We caught a glimpse of something in the rocks ahead,' Blanco told them. 'It might be nothing. It might be an ambush. If it is, it is a good one.'

'We could make a break for that scrub,' Nullo said. 'We just might look a little foolish if there's nothing there.'

'If there is someone there,' Gomez said, 'they could pick us off before we reached it. And when we got there we would be pinned down.'

'We could rush the position,' Blanco said.

'Too steep,' Gomez said. 'We'd be dead before we crawled half-way up.'

'What do you say, Nullo?'

'Head for the scrub.'

'Gomez?'

'Turn and run.'

'We wouldn't make it out of range in time,' Nullo said.

'I say neither run nor hide, since neither will serve us,' Blanco said. 'If our enemy is hiding in those rocks, my children, let us go bravely to meet him. For look: if you face your enemy and curse him even as he kills you, then all he robs you of is your life. But if he kills you running, he steals your life and name too. There the lesson endeth. Evans, you are pale like me.'

'I have my father's Welsh skin, Blanco. It does not brown.'

'Lobo, you tremble.'

'It is with excitement, Blanco.'

'Did I not tell you life would never be dull with Blanco?'

'Porfirio, we shall have to plug your ass. I do not want you to disgrace us.'

Porfirio giggled.

Blanco laughed too, and, spying a fist-sized rock, he picked it up. 'Remove his breeches.'

Everyone laughed now, except Porfirio, who shortly began to scream.

'Good. He is a good screamer. If there are any damned *federales* up there, I hope they have ears to hear with. Let us go.'

They walked forward leading their horses, leaving Porfirio squirming in the dirt. The echoes of his screams came up at them out of the gloom of the river valley.

Nullo heard the zing a split second before the air quivered to the blast. In a moment of dead silence, he watched heads turn, mouths open, hands reach for weapons, all in silence. A pink plume sprang from the head of Miguel. As the particles of brain and blood flew upwards, sound erupted – half a dozen voices shouted at once, while the echo of the rifle boomed through the dead jungle. Blanco started up the rock on the run.

The rock sloped up to a stack of flat-faced boulders. A cloud of smoke, tinted rosy by the low sun, swirled above the boulders. An orange flame flashed in the smoke.

Under the rifle-blast, Nullo heard the bullet crack Gomez's breastbone – like a hammer snapping a slat. Nullo pulled the gun out of his hand even as he went down. Vicente spun round and fell on his back sideways across the slope. There was a hole in his shoulder and his racing heart pumped a spray of blood from it. Three guns going off together made a rat-a-tat and Lobo grabbed at his stomach. His knees gave and he knelt. Nullo flattened himself behind him. Lobo was twitching and trembling. His head hung on his chest and a low clenched-teeth moan came from him.

Five men still ran up the slope. Blanco was in the lead and he hadn't far to go. Evans' head rocked back like he'd taken a slap. Stone dead, he ran on while his legs buckled.

Blanco fell and went rolling down the slope. Toto turned to look and a bullet smashed into his ear. His eyes rolled up until only the whites showed and he began to stagger in Nullo's direction until he stumbled on Evans' body and fell.

Three left now. Up ahead, the Zapotec threw away the club that was his only weapon and squatted down to sing a death chant. Alfonso stumbled on up, screaming from a raw throat and shouldering the useless shotgun he'd taken from Benito the farmer. To Nullo's right and below, Vacca lay behind the dying Vicente. There was a slight dip in the rock just under where Vicente lay and Vacca had flattened himself into it.

Looking back up the slope, he saw Alfonso had decided to retreat. As he ran, the sombrero was whipped forward off his head. The next shot got him and his mouth sprayed teeth and blood. The Zapotec gave an angry grunt and collapsed.

Nullo felt a warmth in his pants. He glanced down, found he hadn't pissed himself after all. It was Lobo's blood, running down between his calves and the soles of his feet. In the cool of the evening, a wisp of steam came off it.

He thought he was hidden from above, but he was afraid that Vacca would call to him and give him away. But Vacca's eyes were fixed on the boulder stack with the rosy smoke swirling above it. He had Jaime Vargas's rifle propped on Vicente's ribs and he waited for a clear shot. He fired and was answered by a shot that gouged his calf. He ducked his head and drew his legs up. But that raised his hips. The rifle blasted and Vacca's poncho twitched over the hip. He tried to flatten his hips and at the same time bend up his calves to the side. He was in bad pain. Nullo could see tears running down his face.

Vicente had stopped squirting blood and lay still. Toto clutched his head and made no sound, but his body trembled. The Zapotec lay with his head below his legs, blinking at the sky.

Vacca yelled:

'You killed my *compañeros*, vermin. You won't kill Vacca. Vacca kills Vacca. See?'

Vacca stuck the barrel of the rifle under his chin. Stretching down made him clench his teeth and groan, but he kept going till he hooked a thumb on the trigger.

'When I get to hell I screw your mother.'

The gun roared and a little volcano of brain and gunsmoke erupted from the top of Vacca's head as the rifle kicked out of his hands. Smoke streamed from his nostrils and mouth and billowed around his head.

The silence seemed to ring.

Nullo crouched behind the kneeling body of Lobo. He thought Lobo was dead now. Anyway, he didn't move. He looked at the gun he had taken from Gomez. He was afraid to break open the chamber in case the noise was heard. There were two bullets that he could see and he hoped there was one under the pin.

He heard what sounded like the crack of a knee joint straightening. A spur chinked and a couple of pebbles rolled down the slope. Nullo listened to the footsteps and kept himself hidden behind Lobo. A little man came in sight. He was about forty-five, with a thin face deeply gouged at the cheeks and a neck you could fit your hand around. A couple of licks of hair striped his bald head. His eyes were two weary slits.

The stranger walked across to Toto and, lowering the barrel of the big Sharps .50 calibre cannon he carried, fired into his head.

Nullo drew a bead and fired. Nothing. The stranger's head snapped round at the strike of the hammer on the pin. Nullo jerked back out of sight.

He listened to the chink of the stranger's spurs. They weren't coming in his direction. When they stopped, Nullo risked another look. The stranger's rifle pointed at the Zapotec's head. As he pulled the trigger, Nullo pulled his. The chamber wheel turned a fraction of an inch then stuck.

The stranger began to walk. Nullo listened to the chink of spurs and the crunch of boot heels. He guessed when the stranger came in sight he might be two dozen feet to his right. Too far to rush him. It was a long throw for a knife. Nullo figured he'd got about a one-in-five chance of hitting him. The odds were longer against hitting him and dropping him.

He brought out the knife and held it with the

91

blade swinging. It had a loud click when it locked, so he would have to lock it on the throw.

A voice spoke in a Texas drawl.

'Hol' hard there, hoss.'

Nullo looked into the barrel of the Sharps.

'You about to cut yourself a chaw, or was you aimin' to sling that thing?'

Nullo let the blade of the knife swing.

'What, this thing? Shoot, I was just lookin' at her. Has sentimental memories. My mamma cut my daddy's throat with it.'

'You from Texas?'

'Washington-on-the-Brazos.'

'Pitch the shiv downhill.'

Nullo tossed the knife away. 'Misfortunate times brung a poorboy this far south of Mason-Dixon, but I b'heve in my heart the Southland shall rise again.'

'What y'all doin' with this scum?'

'Oh, rapin' and pillagin'. You done quizzin' me? Maybe you'd like me to croon "Beautiful Dreamer" before you plug me?'

'I don't reckon so. You can say your prayers if you've a mind.'

'I don't reckon so.'

'Up to you. I got my Bible in my pocket here, and I'll read a text over your body. Mind, the more I see of this here life, the more my faith is shook. But what's a man to do, if he ain't gonna fall to the level of these here? What they done to that old-timer took some believin'. I put him out of his misery on the first shot. Wild beasts is all they is. But . . . I'll say a word over them too – guess it's only right. You want to turn away or see it comin'?'

'I've a notion to look you right in the eye, peckerwood. And I'm gonna hump your momma in hell.'

The little man levelled the Sharps.

The world grew very intense. It felt like staring at the sun.

Eleven

The silence became hard and brittle. Too hard and brittle to exist.

It shattered.

Gramma Bella's grits on his mind. Sowbelly for side-meat Saturday. Chitt'lin's Friday. Wasn't fair this was his last thought. Was there pain to come?

The blast roaring in his ears, Nullo opened his eyes and saw the stranger trying to pull himself out of a sideways stagger. The Sharps lay six feet from him and blood pumped out of his left shoulder.

Blanco was running up the hill. The stranger's feet tangled and he went down and before he could reach the Sharps Blanco was over him and pointing a Colt in his face.

'You want to pray, pus from a leper? You'll pray to God to let you die. First I shoot off your balls, if you have any. You hide up there and kill all my men. Good men. Every one of them better than you. What I wipe from my asshole is better than you.'

Blanco aimed his pistol at the stranger's groin. 'Wait.'

The stranger raised an open palm, gave a twist of the wrist – and there was a Derringer in his hand.

'Better think again, El Blanco. This little thing ain't much more than a pimp's gewgaw, but we're close enough so's it'll pop a hole in your head.'

'Why don't you shoot then? What I got is no toy, my friend. It shoot you with a big hot slug that sears your liver so it sizzles.'

'Shootin's not what I got in mind.'

'Good. I can wait till the leak that you sprung drains you dry.'

'You don't look too watertight yourself.'

Blanco's shirt was soaked with blood from armpit to belt.

'I still got a bucket of blood in me.'

'Not for long. Speakin' personal, I'd rather live myself than see you dead.'

'Death is all in the dying. Without the fear it is nothing. We are both going to die here, *amigo*.'

'That ain't necessarily so. I passed a mission on the way here.'

'So?'

'We both need patching up, and that right quick. I say you put up your gun, I put up mine, and I'll lead you to the mission. We mightn't make it, but you look husky and I take some killin' too.'

Blanco glanced at Nullo.

Nullo stared back blankly for a second – the world still looked a little too bright and hard-edged. 'Makes sense,' he said.

'Better make up your mind quick. Uncock that piece and I'll uncock this'n.'

'All right. No tricks, little man.'

Blanco eased the hammer on his Colt and the stranger did the same.

'You ain't going to make it as far as your horses unless I put a plug to that blood now,' Nullo said.

He stripped the shirts off Alfonso and the Zapotec and did some rough bandaging on Blanco and the stranger. Then he rounded up the horses and helped them mount.

The stranger led them across the river and up out of the gully and they rode east as stars emerged through the pale blue of the sky. When the stars were bright, they came to the edge of the high country, where a steep path wound down round the massive rock faces and then they descended till they reached a bare dry plain. The moon rose over the far sierras and bathed the alkali plain in its beams so it stretched before them like a calm white lake.

'Weak,' Blanco said. 'Feel a chill in my guts too. There are a million stars in the sky, and every one of them will shine when Blanco is gone. Do you believe we exist when we die, Nullo?'

'I don't think about it.'

'I think about it now. That is because I am weak. Weak as a baby. Can hardly close my fist. . . . Ahh, I say damn God.'

The stranger spoke with an effort. 'The fix we're in, you'd be better off praying to God than cursing him.'

'He would not listen to my prayers. Nullo, you pray for me.'

'No use praying to the god I believe in.'

'I have my god too – oh, my head spins – he lives in the *cojones*, and he is a very old god.'

'Just a god of animals,' the stranger said, his voice hitching on the words. 'But there must be something that puts the spark of decency in a man. Too close to the end to fine-sift the arguments . . . so while I still got breath to do it . . . guess I'm gonna bear testimony. . . . There's only one God. His name is Jehovah. He is a just God. And this is his word.' The stranger swayed in his saddle. Nullo reached over, thinking he was going to fall. But the stranger righted himself, drawing as he did a fat little book from his pocket. The moonlight gleamed on the filigreed title of the Bible.

'Hah, we all make our credo tonight.' Blanco coughed and spat. 'Your turn Nullo.'

Nullo reached in his breast pocket. 'My god? He ain't a just god, but he's even, and this is his word.'

Nullo held up his deck and moonlight glinted on the Knave.

'Guess he's smiling on y'all too.' Nullo pointed ahead.

A patch of mesquite scrub and cactus began to show itself over the false horizon of the plain's undulation, and amongst the vegetation they glimpsed the moonlight-stippled tiles of a long low roof and the silhouette of a bell-tower and a cross.

Nullo pounded on one of the two big board-and-brace doors. A sleepy old Indian opened a spy-hatch to their hammering. He disappeared. After ten minutes returned with two monks and the door was opened to them. They were led to a dormitory. Of the six beds, one was occupied by an old woman hacking her lungs out. Two monks bedded Blanco and the stranger down and cleaned and dressed their wounds.

A monk handed Nullo a bowl of bean soup as he lay on his bed.

'Who's in charge of this place?' Nullo asked.

'The superior is Father Kranz. He is not here. He is in the desert.'

'In the desert, huh? What's he doing there?'

'He has been there for three days. It is a penance.'

'What has he done?'

The monk shrugged. He was a chubby monk, with sleek skin and red lips. 'Eh, I do not know.

Father Kranz is a good man. But he thinks too much. He thinks, and discovers sins. Me, I am sure I have more sins than Father Kranz, but I do not look for them.'

'Why did you take our weapons?' Blanco said. He tried to put some gravel in his voice, but he had to pause to catch his breath between words.

'You do not need your weapons. You are safe here.'

'Maybe this Father Kranz is not the only one who is coming. Maybe you sent for the *federales* too.'

'No.' The monk shrugged, but he looked uneasy. 'What need for the *federales*?'

'Do you know who I am?' Blanco demanded.

'No,' the monk said, and his eyes shifted uneasily.

The old woman hacked her dry cough. Nullo could hardly keep his eyes open to finish his soup. He put the bowl to his mouth, gulped it down so that the chilli pepper made his nose run. He wiped his mouth with the back of his hand, used the heel of his thumb on his nose, and felt the bowl being lifted out of his hand as he fell asleep.

In the afternoon quiet, Nullo listened to a horsefly buzz at the shutters, listened to the distant rattle of pots, listened to the creak of the stool as the fat monk shifted his weight. The old woman had hacked herself out for the time being.

The door opened and a tall monk in a black

habit entered. The fat monk stood up and bustled over to him. With the fat monk standing beside him whispering in his ear, Nullo could see that the other monk's height was an illusion. He was about the same height as the fat monk, who wasn't tall, but he was very thin and narrow in the shoulders. He had thin, fine white hair and his skin was white and lifeless. The bones of his face were fine and showed sharp against the skin. His blue eyes were listless.

The fat monk nodded at some command and bustled out, and the thin monk said:

'I am Father Kranz. To this mission I bid you welcome.'

His accent had a familiar ring to Nullo, and he wondered if the monk had any kin in Rosewood. If you strolled across Rosewood County and passed the time of day with everyone you met, one in three would answer you in that choppy Fritz accent. They all had that back-ways style of saying things too.

The stranger hawked the phlegm from his throat and said, 'Thank you for your kindness. Randolph Ransome's my name. And I'm in the employ of the government of the United States. My pale-skinned bedfellow here is none other than the infamous El Blanco. The other goes by the name of Nullo and is his confederate. If you have any law around here, well, I recommend you up and notify it.'

'The *federales* will be notified,' the monk replied.

Blanco raised himself on an elbow. When he spoke there was a hollowness in his voice that told how close death had crept.

'He's crazy, Father. I am not El Blanco. I am a poor peasant. I have the same disease of the skin as the White One, that is all.'

The monk bowed his head and said regretfully, 'Nevertheless, I must notify the *federales*. You have gunshot wounds, and this mission would be closed if I did not tell the police. Please forgive me, my son.'

Blanco cackled. 'Forgive you? Hah. You ask me to forgive you? I flayed a priest once, and stood him in the sun till he crusted over. But since you beg me, all right, I forgive you.'

'Thank you.'

Blanco laughed again. 'You are witty.' Then, his voice become sly, he said, 'Father, will you forgive me something I did?'

The monk bowed his head. His face was drawn with exhaustion, and his meagre frame seemed hardly able to bear the weight of his coarse black habit.

'Come here, I want to whisper.'

The monk went to Blanco and bent over him. Blanco put his cracked lips to the monk's ear and began to whisper. The monk's lips quivered a little at one point, but otherwise his face

remained calm. This seemed to provoke Blanco.
His eyes flashed and he hissed fiercely into the
monk's ear.

Aloud, Blanco said, 'Now do you forgive me?'

'I forgive you,' the monk replied. 'As does Jesus.'

'Get your face away from me. Your breath
stinks of death.'

The monk stepped back. 'I have been fasting. It
makes the breath foul. I am sorry.'

'Sorry? Sorry? What have you to be sorry for? I
have things to be sorry for, but I am not.'

'I will be sorry for you, my son.'

'Ha, ha. I'll laugh my wounds open. Look at you.
I think you have more need of this bed than me.
You have been fasting? For how long?'

'Seven days.'

'Seven days in the desert?' Nullo said.

'The desert is good for the soul.'

'Did the devil tempt you?' Blanco said.

'Yes.'

'What did he tempt you with? Did he offer you
power over all the cities of the world?'

'Yesterday, with a certain recollection, he
tempted me to feel pleasure. On a certain day,
some weeks ago, Brother Eduardo told a joke, and
at his joke no one laughed. Yesterday I remembered this, and the devil tempted me to feel a
pleasure at Brother Eduardo's discomfiture. The
reason for my malice was that Brother Eduardo
had earlier praised my predecessor's Latin

pronunciation, when he knows it is not good, my own pronunciation.'

Blanco cackled until he began to cough. 'You scratch for sins with a fine-tooth comb. Little sins like fleas. What would you do if you had sins like mine – not flea-sins, sins big like tarantulas crawling over you? Could you bear it?'

'I could not bear it. But . . . perhaps God has given to you a soul big enough to bear such sins. . . . Whereas my soul, my soul is a mean soul and weak.' The monk, with his hands clasped to his breast and hidden in the drooping sleeves of the habit, stood and contemplated his imperfections. Then he raised his head and said, 'This mission house and chapel is in honour of Saint Julian called. Julian was a mercenary, and of all who plied the bloody trade, Julian was most sanguinary. He did great evil. His own father and his mother he killed. A destroyer of towns. He killed men, women and the helpless babes too—'

'Babies? I never killed a baby.' Blanco mused. 'And how did he kill them – mercifully?'

'Not mercifully. He said that his lust for cruelty was greater than his lust for women. That it inflamed him more than wine.'

'And they made this – Julian? – a saint? His was a strange piety.'

'Julian repented of his sins. He wandered from town to town in rags with mendicant bowl in hand. And if to him was offered food, he begged to be allowed to share the turnip-peel and cabbage-stalks that to the swine were flung. The repentant tears that Julian shed wore channels in his face from cheek to chin.'

'And they made a saint of him . . .' Blanco repeated.

'It don't seem hardly just he went to heaven after all his depredations,' Ransome said.

'Shut up,' Blanco said. 'What do you know of it?'

'Evil is with goodness twined,' the monk said, 'to make a knot not easy to unpick.'

Twelve

'Why do you want revenge?'

'Because that which was most precious to me was taken from me.'

'And what is that?'

'The woman that I loved. Maria.'

'That is not a good answer. That is a white man's answer. The white men are full of lies. So full of lies that they lie even to themselves. The woman is gone. Killing this man will not bring her back. But something else has been taken from you. Your pride as a man and a warrior has been taken from you.'

'I am not a proud man and I am not a warrior. It is for Maria.'

'So, you keep beating this white man's drum. The woman is no more. But there are other women. Only – a man who has been defeated will not have his pick of the other women. It is no excuse that you were outnumbered and defenceless. Fortune has shown her scorn for you. If you prove you have strength, you will win her again. The gods despise weakness and love strength. This, now, is a good reason for revenge.'

Jaime felt his eyes sting. He could have wished for something other than this from Lame Deer. Yesterday he'd thought of tying a rope to the jacaranda tree. If he could have chosen life or death without having to think about the mechanics of ending his life, he would not be here now. But suicide takes an effort of will, and his will was mush. So he'd sat under the tree in a stupor, until he grew ashamed of his docility, which was an insult to Maria, and eventually he wound himself up to a pitch where he did hang a noose from a branch. But, he thought, if he could find suicide in him, perhaps there was fire enough in his belly for something more difficult. If his spirit were of a man's temper, he would take revenge for his wife. With his mind fixed on this, he had come to Lame Deer, whose dead brother had been Maria's father, but instead of the help he sought he found arguments to baffle his brain, which was already baffled sufficiently.

'These reasons are not my reasons. My reason is Maria.'

'This is too much talk. And it is white man's talk, which means little. But if you have a good reason your actions will prove it. So, go with your white man's reason and take your revenge.'

'I have no chance against this man. That is why I came to you.'

'You do not believe in the red man's reason, but you believe in his power.'

'I believe in his power. I am half an Indian myself.'

'Good. We will see what can be done with this half. First you must feed the dog of revenge.'

Lame Deer took a hunting knife from his belt and placed it on the rush mat on which they sat.

'If you have a good reason, we will soon know. You will be left alone here for a day and a night. Look up there.'

Lame Deer pointed up at the wall of the tepee. On the hide was painted an eagle with pinions spread above the prostrate figure of a puma-headed man. The eagle's talons pulled a string of intestines from the man's guts.

'Just before the sun hides behind the sierras, it will shine through a hole in the hide into the bowels of the cat god. Tomorrow at sunset I will bring the dog and we will see if you have something to offer him.'

Jaime knew that Lame Deer was giving him time to think. But it was an insult to Maria to think. In honour of his love, he should cut now and sit here and suffer the pain till tomorrow night. He lifted the knife from the mat. The edge was scoured bright by the whetstone. He put his thumb to the edge. It still had the slight, ragged burr that showed it had not cut since sharpening. It produced a ticklish sensation in his thumb, like pins and needles. The sensation passed from his thumb along his arm and down into his stomach. He threw the knife down on the mat – when it was in his hand he could think of nothing but it.

Maria's face came to his mind. Jaime's heart swelled, swelled as if it would burst his chest. Tears started to his eyes. He snatched up the knife.

The hide-wrapped haft felt weighty in his hand. The blade was thick on the back edge and heavy enough to balance the haft.

His love was great . . . but the knife was sharp.

Their marriage had not been completely as he would have wished. He'd wanted the freedom and openness of friendship. She wanted something that had to do with fear and need. There were times when she'd humiliated him. She had to, before she could love him. She resented him – because he was a man, and according to the world her superior. And she resented even the fact that she loved him and therefore her happiness depended on him. But it was because she loved him that she paid him the thorny compliment of resentment.

The day grew cool and the women called the children to dinner.

There were two forces opposed: his idealism and the knife. His idealism was large, but it was formless, ungraspable: whereas, though the knife was little enough to be held in the hand, still it most definitely could be held in the hand, and its form was very distinct.

Ah, there is no doubting the knifeness of this knife, Jaime thought.

The sun set. Jaime did not sleep, but after a fashion he dreamed. In his waking dream he witnessed a violent struggle. Two forces fought, and as they fought they changed shape. At one point a man with a sword fought a spectre. The swordsman could not stab the spectre, but the spectre, being a thing without material substance, could not harm the swordsman. The swordsman became a wolf and it waged a great and futile conflict with the sea. The forces changed their shape, became no shape, but the struggle went on. It seemed to him now that reality fought with unreality. When the cock crew for morning, the struggle still raged, and to Jaime it felt that his mind fought for its reason. Then while the walls of the tent grew light, all his failings joined forces to struggle against his belief in himself, and with burning cheeks he hung his head and wished that he did not exist, and wished that there never had existed the being that was Jaime Vargas.

Enough, he thought. There is the knife, of which there is no question. The thing that is in question is my love for the memory of Maria. But it seems it shrinks from the proof.

'It is not love I need now, but hate.'

He lifted the knife and the blade, glimmering in the dawn twilight, seemed to his half-dreaming mind to have the look of a mouth stretched in a sardonic grimace.

'You grin, knife?'

He turned the blade slightly so the glimmer disappeared.

'What will defeat you, if neither love nor hate?'

'No answer? But of course you can't talk, so how can you answer? The answer is within myself, and I will find it or I will not find it. It is very simple if you do not think.'

The day wore on and sun crept towards the western sierras. All the objects in the tepee took the evening look of tarnished brass. Jamie raised his eyes to the eagle. A ray of sunlight pierced a hole in the tepee and lit the eagle and the disembowelled god. The eagle's pinions glowed like twin flames.

It is all nonsense – love, hate, pride, revenge – all nonsense. Jaime raised the knife. So why, he wondered as he put the edge to the V of his ear, am I doing this nonsense?

'It is to honour the great god of nonsense,' he said and drew the blade through skin into gristle.

'And there . . . oh, God . . . there he is.'

The muzzle of a black dog had appeared through the slit of the tent. It fixed its eyes with keen interest on the blood running down Jamie's cheek. Jamie continued to draw the knife backwards and forwards. The dog whimpered. Jaime whimpered too.

As long as Jamie's agonized breathing sounded, Lame Deer held the dog back.

'Come,' Jaime gasped.

Lame Deer pulled back the flap of the tepee and entered with the dog.

'See?' Jaime held out his dripping ear. His hand and arm shook like a reed in strong wind.

Lame Deer nodded. 'Let us see if the god of revenge is hungry.'

'There.' Jaime threw the ear on to the mat. 'Gobble it up.'

Lame Deer released the dog. It padded over to the ear and sniffed it.

'Will you turn up your nose at an ear?' Jaime said. 'It is a good ear. A fresh ear. Eat my ear, oh god of fleas.'

'Do not speak lightly,' Lame Deer said.

The dog made a snatch at the ear and picked it up in its teeth. It jerked the ear into its mouth and began to gnaw.

It was as if a strong hand gripped Jamie's backbone and gave it a brief violent shake.

Lame Deer's wife, Consuela, slipped into the tent and began to wash and apply ointment to Jaime's wound. His head felt twice its normal size and burned like fire even with the cooling ointment.

'When you are healed, we will go into the mountains,' Lame Deer said.

'Until then, I will chant. I will pray to the spirits and try to turn them against the spirit of this man. How is he called?'

'His name is Nullo,' Jaime said.

Thirteen

Benito sat in Jaime Vargas's soot-blackened cottage. It did not shelter him from the sun – the roof timbers had been burnt and the roof had collapsed – but the adobe walls still stood and they kept off some of the wind. Benito's own wooden shack had been razed to the ground. From time to time he would make plans for the future and, full of nervous energy, his spirits would lift for a while, but mostly it was enough for him to do to light the fire and cook up his mess of beans.

Let's face it, Benito thought, my life has been destroyed. Since the age of twelve I have laboured in the fields. I am used up, and have not the strength to start over. The woman and the girl were a help in the work and company in the house, but now I am on my own. God has decreed it so. Perhaps He will give me reason to live, or maybe He will let me die. I do not know what His plans are. Jaime has beans and hominy. There is pulque too, but drink has never made me cheerful.

One day, he heard a slap of sandals on the dirt path. People had come before, but he had hidden from them. Quite why, he did not know. Perhaps he had just been too dispirited to speak to anyone. Anyway, they did not like him in the village. Because he was silent and drove a hard bargain. Now they would be sorry for him, but he felt in a corner of their hearts they would also gloat to see him brought low.

Juárez the carpenter stepped through the charred frame of the doorway. He had his shotgun over his shoulder and his game bag slung from his neck.

'Benito, we have been looking for you. The *federales* have been looking for you.'

'What do the *federales* want with me?'

'They want to question you – you and Jaime Vargas. They found the grave here, and the two graves at your own farm, and they guessed that you and Jaime each must have buried your dead. Where is Jaime?'

'I do not know.'

'There is a rumour that he has gone looking for Blanco?'

'Who – Jaime?'

'I do not believe it myself.'

Juárez stood looking down at him. Benito thought if he stayed any longer he would have to

114

share his beans with him.

'Oh, why do you not come to town?'

'For what?'

'At a time like this you need the consolation of friends.'

Benito grunted.

'There is news of El Blanco. The *federales* say he is at the mission of the Capuchins, over in Matapec.'

'If they know where he is, why do they not arrest him?'

'They cannot touch him. He has been given sanctuary. He has become a monk. *Dios*, this world is a strange place.'

'Not so strange. Blanco is shrewd.' Benito felt a swelling of his heart and he said: 'Will you lend me your gun?'

Juárez looked uneasy. Benito knew what was on his mind. He was afraid if he lent his gun he would never see it again.

'The consolation of friends is all very well, but when it comes to risking your gun, that is something else.'

'But it will do no good for you to get killed yourself.'

'Let me worry about that. Are you going to lend it to me?'

'Look, I am going hunting now. I will pass this way again at sunset. That will give you time to think about this less rashly. If you are still firm,

115

then I will leave you the gun. But you should forget revenge. It is in the hands of God now, and if Blanco has genuinely reformed you would only thwart God's purpose. If I were you I would go to the mine. The Dutchman is hiring – labourers and carpenters. The Dutchman won't have me, because of taking that little bit of lumber last time I worked there. But you should go. Tell them you are a carpenter. You are good enough. Might as well get the two pesos more. I will leave you now, Benito, and say goodbye until this evening.'

But Juárez did not come back in the evening.

Benito felt a little relieved. He did not quite know what had prompted him to ask for the gun. Perhaps it had been a touch of bravado. He had not thought of going after Blanco before, and he did not want to now. But it began to prey on his mind. Juárez would tell them how he'd asked for the gun and how he, Juárez, had saved him from himself. They would probably think his asking was only big talk, and that he was relieved he did not get it.

Still, what did he care what they thought or what they said?

But it did bother him. It began to bother him more and more. They didn't like his stubbornness. And it would give them satisfaction to see that when it came to man's work he wasn't as stubborn as he was when driving a bargain over the price of seed. He would like to show them that he was not like them, that when he said something it was not for the sake of flapping his tongue.

The trouble was, Blanco would probably kill him. Well, that was one solution to his problems. Anyway, he did not have a gun. He supposed if he was stubborn enough he would go after him with his bare hands, or his machete. He wondered what it would be like to take a cut at a man with a machete. If it came to it, Blanco would no doubt put a bullet in him before he got close enough to find out. Then he remembered what Juárez had said about the Dutchman hiring. If he could get work at the mine, after a couple of weeks he could buy a gun.

And get himself killed.

He did not make a conscious decision to go after Blanco, but the idea began to work on his mind as a fever works on the body. Next day he was still in a turmoil, and after eating his meal of beans he could not sit still. He jumped to his feet, and without thinking about it any more, he headed out for the mine.

To his surprise, there was a job for him. Fortune was either paying off the arrears of luck it had withheld all his miserable life, or smoothing the way for his suicide. The Dutchman gave him a hammer and a saw and put him to work with three other carpenters to build some huts on piecework, paid by the foot of timber. Benito put his head down, ignored his workmates, and set to work. When the others knocked off he worked on, and was still working by the light of the full moon. He felt they looked at him as you would look at someone who had leprosy. Benito did not want sympathy, but that look they gave him – the Dutchman included – from the corners of their eyes, from under their brows, annoyed him. Benito was not to blame for his tragedy, no more than the leper for his disease, but still he got that look. Well, let them look how they liked and let them think what they wanted. If he was a rich man lazing in the lap of fortune, no doubt they would be all smiles. But he was a poor man, spat on by fortune and pissed on too, and if that embarrassed them and if the sight of him labouring like an ox disgusted them, then that was too bad. Benito finished his work in two weeks while the others still had at least half a week's work to do. He drew his wages and bought a Springfield rifle from the mining company's store.

Fourteen

'Drink this,' Lame Deer commanded.

Jaime took the bowl of mud-coloured liquid and put it to his lips. It had an old, earthy taste. If a dry corpse were powdered and an infusion made of it, it might taste like this. But a person capable of lopping off his own ear had no business turning finicky over a drink, so Jaime swallowed it.

'Put your trust in me,' Lame Deer said as he led him to a tree that stood at the cliff's edge. 'You must trust me. Do you trust me?'

'I trust you,' Jaime mumbled. Already light-headed from the billowing smoke Lame Deer had caused by sprinkling powders on the fire, the disgusting drink was making him reel.

'You must trust me,' Lame Deer said as he tied Jaime to the tree with hide strips. He tied him at the ankles and stretched his arms back over his head and tied them by the wrists.

'Do you trust me?'

'I . . .' Jaime nodded. He could hardly heave in a breath.

Jaime lost sight of Lame Deer behind the billows of dirty smoke that rolled off the fire.

Lame Dear reappeared with his spear in his hand.

'You must trust me.'

Lame Deer lunged at Jaime.

'Do you trust me?'

His skin popped. Jaime watched the stretched skin tear wider the puncture in his belly. The spear's shaft was lost in his gut.

'You've killed me,' Jaime said and turned his amazed eyes up to Lame Deer's.

'But you are still alive,' Lame Deer said, and twisted the spear.

Jaime howled in agony.

'Now I will kill you.'

Jaime's guts felt like a bucket of hot tar that was being given a stir with a stick. Right up his backbone, up to his skull-bone he felt a grating – he heard it inside him.

The point scraped Jaime's backbone, found a crevice that fitted it, and Lame Deer put the weight of his shoulder to the shaft.

The light snuffed out in Jaime's head.

There were rocks and sky and wind. He was dead. But that seemed like something that happened a long time ago. Lame Deer was there. And he was there too, drooping from the tree. But he didn't pay much attention to himself or Lame Deer. The rocks and grass and trees were just as important. He felt nothing. Felt no more than the grass did. Lame Deer moved about busily. But what he was doing had no interest for him. Nothing interested him in this place. Yet he did not want to leave and go someplace else. He had no desire to leave or stay. He wanted nothing. It was strange to want nothing, but it did not bother him. This was how the rocks felt. And he could squat here like a rock for a million years and it would not bother him. Life was a fever: it had abated and did not bother him any more.

Something began to bother him. Lame Deer's voice bothered him a lot. He wanted Lame Deer to go away. He wanted it more than anything in the world. He wanted a drink too. And he wanted these thoughts out of his head. Thoughts whirled in his brain like wreckage in a whirlwind.

'You must trust me. Do you trust me?'

'What. . . ? What do you want? What do . . .'

Jaime looked down at his body. There was no mark on it. He was sitting by the fire and he wanted to move back because it was too hot. But he wanted to move closer too, because his back was cold.

'I want—'

'That's right. You are alive. So you want. That is what it means to live. But you see how foolish it is? A child wants a toy gun. He wants it with all his soul. But when he is a boy, he wants a real rifle. He scorns the toy and cannot believe he wanted it so much. When he is a man he wants a woman. And when that fierce wanting is gone from him, he remembers it with wonder. When you were dead you wanted nothing.'

'It's true. Nothing. It is pointless to want things. I remember now.'

'That's right. You were dead. And now you do not fear death, because you see how little importance life has. Is that not right?'

'It's right.'

'What do you desire?'

'Nothing.'

'Then why live?'

'I don't know.'

'But you must desire if you want to live. You desire the death of the man called Nullo. That is your one desire. That is the reason you live. Now you must repeat.'

Lame Deer spoke strange words. Jaime repeated them. He had to repeat them till he got them right, and then he had to repeat them over and over. He sang till the words ran together and as he sang the words, he felt the radiance of his spirit concentrate into a point of light. He felt that this light had terrible power, that if he focused it on something he could annihilate it. He felt that if he tried hard and reached a single moment of perfect focus, he could blast even the earth apart, send its fragments whirling among the stars.

'Sleep, Jaime,' Lame Deer said.

Jaime slept.

'Wake up,' Lame Deer said.

Jaime woke.

'I have food for you. Are you hungry?'

Jaime smiled. 'Am I hungry? Like the lean wolf whose belly cleaves to his spine, oh Uncle.' Jaime was generally happy for a few moments on wakening. Until he remembered Maria.

'This is. . . .'

'Tasty?'

'I have no words,' Jaime said as he worried the crisp-skinned flesh off the turkey-cock. 'You are truly a great shaman.'

'You have to cook a bird on a hot fire,' Lame Deer said, ripping at a leg with his teeth. 'It is a mistake to cook it too slow. Lose too much juice. I stuff the belly with hominy too. So the fat will soak in and not drip away. More?'

'*Dios* . . . save the bones, I will crunch them later.'

After they had eaten, Lame Deer made a cigarette and passed his tobacco-pouch to Jaime.

'Ah, life is good, is it not?'

'I had some very strange dreams,' Jaime said.

'Dreams?'

Jaime paused with the cigarette at his lips, looked curiously at Lame Deer.

123

'Are you sure you are not dreaming now?' Lame Deer said.

'I never ate in a dream.'

'Did you ever eat so well waking?' Lame Deer threw his cigarette into the fire. 'Get up, Jaime.'

Obediently, Jaime stood. Lame Deer took out his knife. The same that had removed Jaime's ear. He pointed to a tree.

Jaime took hold of the knife by the blade. 'I cannot throw a knife.'

He threw the knife at the tree. It struck flat on and bounced.

'See?'

'Try again.'

This time the knife missed the tree by six inches. Jaime searched for it in the bushes.

'I will need a gun,' he said ruefully as he gave back the knife.

'I will give you my Winchester,' Lame Deer said.

Jaime felt what he wanted was a club. A pick-handle. He would grip it till the knuckles whitened and swing with all his strength so it landed sideways to the skull of the whore's dropping that called itself Nullo.

'A club is what I want.' The words bruised his tight throat.

'Control your anger. You must be sharp not blunt.'

Lame Deer took a stick from the fire. With the burnt end of the stick he drew an oval on the tree. It was about the size of a man's head and the same height from the ground. He came back and stood before Jaime, looked in his eyes, said something he did not understand, in a language he did not understand. Lame Deer stepped aside and Jaime saw Nullo.

Lame Deer tossed the knife. It made a lazy loop and Jaime reached up and picked it out of the air. The air whooshed as his arm swung down. The blade drove straight through the bone of Nullo's skull in the space that separates the eyebrows.

Except it wasn't Nullo. The knife stuck in the middle of the charcoal circle Lame Deer had traced on the tree. It was buried the length of half his thumb in the bole and Jaime had to work the handle to pull it out.

'You can't throw a knife?'

'That did not feel like throwing a knife. That was like putting on my sombrero. I just knew how to do it. But to say I knew . . . it is like saying the sea knows how to make a wave. Let me try again.'

Jaime held the knife by the handle as he had before and drew back his arm. But it was all wrong. That sensation of lightness in the muscles, then the wave-smooth acceleration, the unstoppable crescendo . . . all were gone . . . . The knife bounced off the tree-bole into the grass.

Lame Deer said, 'When Nullo stands before you, you will strike like a snake. Do not worry about that or think about it. You must trust me. Do you trust me?'

125

'I trust you.'

'I too have had a dream, Jaime. I dreamed that you met this man and killed him.'

'Killed him. . . .'

'You killed him, but he also killed you. Life is good, Jaime.'

'Do you want me to live?'

'It is also good to die gloriously.'

'I never thought about glory before. I was happy with Maria.'

'Of course, life is mean without glory. But still life is good. Listen to the birds twitter in the fading light. Remember how the charred meat smelt when you were hungry? Smell the earth smells – there are ocelot-droppings in those bushes, and over there I believe a pine is oozing sap.'

'If I was a child or an old man . . . or a woman . . . these things would give me more pleasure.'

'There is no glory or honour in an easy life. But you say you are not concerned about glory or honour.'

Jaime pointed to the scabbed-over wound on the side of his head. 'I have proved myself. I am not the boy I was before. Why do you doubt me?'

Jaime could have wished that he did not doubt himself, or the course he had chosen.

'The old woman who was sick, the mother of Macaw, she is better. I said it was her time to die. But Macaw prides herself on her woman's heart, and she sent her to the mission of the Capuchins, and now she has returned cured. Your enemy is there, at the mission of the Capuchins.'

Fifteen

'Turn over, so I can wipe your ass.'

Ransome's stump waggled. Sometimes he forgot his left arm was buried in the mission graveyard and he tried to move it.

'Should have done it before I took the pan away,' Blanco said as he scrubbed Ransome's buttocks with a moist rag. 'Now it will dirty the sheet. Can't be helped.' He showed Ransome the contents of the pan. 'I like your shit better today. A little firmer.'

The door of the dormitory opened and Father Kranz entered.

'Do I have to be nursed by this?' Ransome asked weakly.

'Brother Pedro himself requested this task.'

Blanco had also requested to adopt the name Pedro, rather than use his own Christian name – Eugenio – because he said San Pedro was number one of the saints.

'The bastard's got a sense of humour. He's laughing at me, and you too.'

'Do not fret, someone else will nurse you. I have for Brother Pedro another task. My son, I want you to accompany me on a journey. A difficult journey it will be. Across the desert, a week's trek. We have no burro, I gave it to the old Mescalero woman to carry her back to her village.'

'No need for a burro, Father,' Blanco said. 'I will be your burro.'

'You must be crazy, going into the desert with him. You'll not come out of it alive.'

'I am not crazy. Simply, I trust God. And I trust that his spirit moves in Brother Pedro.'

Ransome grunted. 'Well, you can take my horse, then. I guess Brother Pedro can walk.'

'Thank you, but you will need it yourself. I have ordered that you be sent to the hospital in Santa Matilda when you are well enough to ride. Perhaps in one more week you will be fit to make the journey.'

'Nullo will wipe your ass when I am gone, won't you Nullo?' Blanco said. 'Unless you want to come with us. Why not take Nullo with us, Father?'

'He can come if he wants. But for you it is a penance and for me it is my work.'

'You stay here, son,' Ransome said. 'I relish the chance to chew the fat with a fellow Texan without the albino butting in.'

The look Ransome gave him told Nullo it was an order and not a request. He was in no position to disobey. The *federales* had to grin and bear it in the matter of Blanco, but they'd claimed that Nullo was not entitled to sanctuary because he wasn't Catholic. It was Ransome who'd stopped them hauling Nullo back to jail – by putting him under arrest. He'd shown them a letter from their chief of police, and that settled the matter. All they could do was confiscate Nullo and Blanco's horses. At least the damned horses cannot claim sanctuary, they'd said. So if Ransome said stay, he stayed. It didn't matter. He'd take a trip into the desert one of these days. It wouldn't go away.

'I'll stay, but I ain't wiping your ass.'

'Where do we go, Father?' Blanco asked.

'There is a company working in the desert. They mine the gypsum dunes. Some men of the Tarahumara tribe have been working in this place, and one of them came today to say his son is gravely injured. He was in a fight and he was shot. I must see if I can help him. And if not, bury him like a Christian and the prayers for the dead say. The young man's father will not return with us, for the journey here has taken all his strength. So, Brother Pedro, we shall start at once, for there is no time to lose. Three days' walk will bring us to a water-hole, but we must carry enough to get us there.'

'I am ready, my teacher. Look after my patient,

130

Nullo.' Blanco turned to Ransome. 'Goodbye, my friend. The Blanco that robbed you of your arm is gone. Before you stands Brother Pedro, a repentant sinner who thinks only of his death and the judgment to come and who begs your forgiveness.'

Ransome let the lids droop over his fever-dulled eyes and gave a grunt for answer.

A cantina and a store and half a dozen clapboard shacks squatted in the desert. The sun glared on the tin roofs of the shacks, and the wind moaned in off the desert and sifted a fine white haze of dust over everything.

A man with sunken, slitted eyes and a scar on his high cheekbone sat in the cantina with a bottle of tequila before him on the table. He sat there every day. Unless you mined the gypsum there was nothing else to do here. He'd come from Sorano where he'd worked for six months in the silver-mine. Every day he grew more irritable, and he did not know why he stayed.

He stayed because he liked being irritable. Up at the silver-mine he'd been even-tempered. There were some tough characters up there, and an irritable man could get himself in trouble. Here there was nothing but some peaceable Indians and he could be as irritable as he wanted. The man drank and stared irritably out of the window.

For a moment he thought he was looking at two ghosts floating out of the desert, and it caused him a funny little sensation, like the beginning of a giggle. It was a pair of monks, he realized, white with dust from the hems of their skirts to the points of the cowls that covered their heads. He watched them shuffle past the cantina. They went into one of the shacks. It was the shack were the Indian he'd shot lay dying.

When he was sober he worried about the Indian. Killing a man was not like stamping on a beetle, and it took some getting used to the idea. Drunk, he felt good. A man is what he does. If he does nothing, his life's a dull story, not worth the telling.

This Indian had laughed in an easy way. Up at the silver-mine there were some who could laugh like that and some who couldn't. Up there if you laughed like that some people would want to know what made you think you could laugh like you hadn't a worry in the world. He hadn't laughed like that himself up at the mine. He'd shot the Indian, just like Montado had shot the man who talked too loud when he was trying to sleep.

After an hour, the monks came out of the shack and went into the store.

If Montado were here now, he would have something to say about the monks. What he admired about Montado was that he didn't need any excuse. If Montado didn't like somebody, that was their fault, and they weren't going to escape just because they stayed out of his way.

Nullo

He often tried to guess what Montado would think or how he would act in a situation. Sometimes he spoke as Montado spoke or imitated the way he walked. The man knocked back another shot of tequila and slammed the glass on the table.

The Indian sitting behind the bar raised his head and looked out from under his sombrero. The stool fell as the man stood. The Indian's dark eyes showed no expression, and after a couple of seconds the sombrero sank to his chest again.

Sixteen

'Each man a prisoner, dragging the chain and ball of his personality, hating the particular chafe of his chain, and envying even the chains of his fellows. Every man would be his opposite.'

'No, my Father, I may want to be you, but how can you want to be me? Do you desire to drink and fornicate and shed blood?'

'Why . . . do you imagine I am proud of this bloodless husk that is Kranz?'

Before entering the store, Brother Kranz uncovered his head – but laid a hand on Blanco's arm as he was about to do likewise. 'Keep you hooded, my son. Your fame is great, and your face is distinctive.'

It was a dim little cabin with the merchandise crowding the floor: stacks of canned food, tin buckets and rush brooms, ground maize and beans in sacks. In the corner beside the counter a woman worked the treadle of a loom. The whirring of the loom slowed, rattled to a stop, and the woman rose and went to her counter.

'*Buenos días,*' the brother superior said. 'We have need of some items – for the young man, Julio, who is injured. Gauze we need, for bandaging. And alcohol, for his wound is suppurating. And have you wych-hazel? Good, good. It is the best thing for soothing the inflamation.'

The woman gathered the things and laid them out on the counter. Brother Kranz opened his purse.

'There is no charge, *Padre.*'

'Thank you, my daughter.' The monk made his humble bow.

The woman lowered her head to conceal her smile. While Blanco gathered the goods, she stole a look at the brother superior.

Her face, framed in its black mantle, was care-worn, but the little light that found this dim corner touched it softly. Her eyes lingered tenderly on the monk's ascetic face. Glancing up, Kranz met her gaze and a spot of colour touched his pale cheek.

'Thank you, thank you,' he repeated . . . and then, softly, with sincere feeling, 'Thank you, my daughter.'

As they left, Blanco, who had missed nothing, muttered, 'You are like me, as I was before – you take for nothing. Only you need no gun.'

'She is a good woman,' the monk muttered in reply.

A tall man with a scarred cheek stood in the blowing dust of the street. His eyes were fixed on them. Brother Kranz stopped and returned his look, but perceiving the ill intent of the other's stare, the monk bowed his head and continued on his way.

'I wish to confess,' the man said.

Brother Kranz hesitated, and Blanco, walking behind with his cowl blown over his eyes, stumbled against him.

'Will you hear my confession?'

'I have a patient that I must attend. If you—'

'That is what I want to confess,' the man said, walking towards them. 'It is my bullet in that village Indian. Won't he die? And what is this, and this?'

The man snatched the roll of gauze from Blanco.

The brother superior touched Blanco's arm. The man noticed the sudden flexing of Blanco's squat body under the habit. For a moment his eyes looked uncertain, then they hardened.

'You try to patch him up, eh? You want to waste a good bullet?'

He tossed the bandage over his shoulder.

Blanco stood with his cowled head bowed for some seconds, then he started over to where the gauze had fallen. The man, as Blanco passed, lifted his boot, placed it low on Blanco's back and shoved. Blanco tottered forward, tangled his legs in his robe, and went sprawling in the dust.

Brother Kranz hurried to him.

'Do not retaliate. It is . . .'

In the shadow of the cowl, the monk caught a glimpse of Blanco's eyes; his hand recoiled. He felt like a rabbit gazing into the eye of a jaguar.

He watched Blanco gather himself, watched, wide-eyed and appalled, the smile that crept over his face.

A fine equilibrium existed in the character of Kranz: his nature, sensitive and timid, had for counterpoise a spirit of the purest temper. With trembling fingers, he reached out and placed his hand on Blanco's clenched fist.

'Whatever he does, you must bear. You must bear the blow and give thanks to Jesus for it. For this is what Julian did.'

The good man was to bear the next blow himself. A kick in the back laid him in the dust. The man went after Brother Kranz – some intuition warned him clear of Blanco – and hauled him to his feet. The monk would not raise his head and this annoyed the man. He'd never landed a square punch on a man's chin before, and he wanted to try his skill with the knockout blow. As it was he had to make do with an uppercut to the face. But he brought it up almost from the ground, straightening his knees as he came up, and finishing with a little jump. The monk's fine nose cracked and the man felt the keen satisfaction of a job well done.

The monk's expression amused him. Just a few minutes ago he'd looked very clever and dignified, now he looked like a child that's just been punished and thinks it's all so unfair. The unfairness was the beauty of it. All their talk of fairness was the biggest swindle of the lot – exactly as if they threw you a manacle and said, 'Here, chain yourself. Save us the trouble.'

Father Kranz raised his bloody face to look, not at the man, but at Blanco. The man glanced round, saw the other on his hands and knees. He looked like a dog about to spring. Or about to bolt. With his face hidden in the shadow of that cowl you couldn't read his intention.

'Thank you, my son.'

The man turned back and stared in amazement at this monk whose blood was sprinkling the dust. He thought he would perish – he was red-faced and sightless before he could spew out the laughter that choked him.

'It was nothing. In fact, since you like it so much, here is more of it.'

Father Kranz hunched his narrow shoulders and tried to duck the fist. It smashed into the side of his head and knocked him to his knees. He drew up his hood, and using one hand to hold it across his face, he knelt in the dust and made no further effort to protect himself.

The man punched and kicked the frail body until a wide swing connected with nothing and strained his elbow tendon. It spoiled his mood and he decided he was ready for a drink. He rounded off his performance with a solid kick to the stomach. The monk retched into his hood.

At the door of the cantina the man stopped. He felt he should say something. He had a moment of inspiration.

'If your Jesus was here I would do the same for him.'

It was a good thing to say – defiant – a challenge to God.

The squat monk was looking at him. At least, he thought he was. He couldn't see his face for the shadow of that cowl – the damned, weird-looking thing. He turned away quickly and went into the cantina.

Blanco helped Brother Kranz back to the shack where the wounded boy lay. He bathed his face and bandaged his ribs and made a bed from sacking for him to lie on. Then he went to the well and scrubbed the brother superior's habit clean of blood and vomit. When he came back he squatted by the wall and watched his monk until the men came back from working at the dunes.

'Have I your permission to go out for a little while?'

'Yes, Brother Pedro . . . but, you are not—'

'I swear to you I will not lay a finger on that man.'

Blanco closed the door and turned towards the cantina.

The man with the scar sat brooding over his tequila. He did not look round when the door opened. Four Indians sat at a table with bowls of pulque before them. Something in their expression made the man turn and he saw the cowled figure of the monk. The monk sat down at a table and the man knocked back his tequila and reached for the bottle. He wondered if this monk was perhaps a little crazy. He filled his glass then turned and took another look at him.

Blanco drew the hood off his head.

The man turned back and reached for his drink. When he touched the glass the liquid began to shimmer. He had filled the glass too full, and he did not trust himself to bring it to his lips without spilling. So he opened his fingers and let the glass sit. A little while later, he closed his fingers round it again. But when he touched it, the shimmer of the liquid was even more violent. A little of it spilled over the side of the glass. So he opened his fingers again and sat looking at the glass.

The Indian who kept the bar stood beside Blanco and said softly, for the third time, '*Señor?*'

'Water,' Blanco said.

Then he looked at the man.

Aware Blanco's eyes were on him, the man grew confused and without thinking lifted the glass. Tequila slopped on to the table. Now he had lifted it he thought the best thing was to bring it quickly to his lips so the shaking of the glass might not be so obvious. The rim of the glass struck his teeth and tequila spilled on the table. Some of it splashed his chin and a little went into his mouth. Now there was the problem of swallowing it, and this he found he could not do. So he held the tequila in his mouth. It became difficult to breathe. It seemed if he did not get a breath he would suffocate. Feeling panic near, he acted decisively: he sniffed in air, but succeeded in breathing in some tequila as well. He spluttered, then coughed.

Tequila came out of his nostrils. His eyes welled up with tears and his nose ran, and the more he tried to control his breathing the more ragged it became.

His face burned red. The Indians' eyes were fixed on him. His own eyes bulged and rolled in the sockets. He was not trembling, but shuddering. His legs jumped and his arms jerked in a way he'd never before experienced or seen. He no longer controlled his own body and he dreaded what it might make him do – fall out of his chair, lose control of his bowels – something dreadful and shameful.

Maybe if he just got up, Blanco would let him leave. But could he walk? And was Blanco going to let him go? After what he had done? The Blanco who killed like a devil? The stories they told – he couldn't think of them . . . now he began to weep silently.

Afterwards he could never understand why he did not make a break for the door instead of doing what he did next. If, while remembering, he could have experienced the same pitch of terror, he might have had an inkling. At the time, one of the notions that went through his head was that Blanco might be sorry. If he saw what he had driven him to, it might make him feel bad. This, feeble as it was, was the only retaliation he had in mind, for when he reached for his gun it was with the idea of putting a bullet in his own brain.

His hand could hardly grip the gun, but somehow he wrenched it out of its holster. Then the thought, like a bolt of lightning, flashed in his brain:

What if Blanco believed he meant to shoot him?

The gun dropped from his hand.

Then his control of himself did give way completely. He fell to his hands and knees, and began to inch along the floor. Every second he expected to feel the hand of Blanco grab him. And he sobbed. He sobbed out loud and did not try to restrain it, because he thought Blanco might be appeased if he sobbed loud enough. The door was almost within reach of his hand. His sobbing took on a new whining note of misery because he knew that Blanco was only tantalizing him. And now his time was run out because he was almost at the door. And so he stopped, because he knew the moment he touched the door it was over.

He was dimly aware of the door opening, and a pair of feet – a woman's feet perhaps, but all was as uncertain as in a dream – were before his eyes.

Then, in the depths of his shame he found some courage in his heart. He would not lie here helpless, and wait for Blanco to take him. He would show Blanco that he was man enough to act. He would struggle for his life to the last, and perhaps Blanco would respect him for it. He gathered all his will-power and jumped to his feet and brushing the woman aside fled past her into the night.

The woman stood in the doorway with a dish of stew in her hands. She'd forgotten the food, as she'd forgotten why she'd come here. She was unconscious too of the expression on her face as she gazed at Blanco.

'You had another look for my brother today.' Blanco picked the gun off the floor.

'One look for Kranz, another for Blanco. I know that look of old. Before I was old enough to know right from wrong, I knew that look. Tell me, what was I to do with such looks – bow my head, say, "Yes, you are right, I am a loathsome white slug?"' Blanco turned to the Indian who kept the bar. 'I would like some brandy. But I have no money.'

The Indian brought a bottle and a glass from under the bar.

143

'There are women who would spit on Kranz and grovel at the feet of Blanco.'

The Indian brought the brandy and the glass down and set them before Blanco.

'Why do you give me brandy? Because of this?'

Blanco laid the gun on the table.

'Your look, woman – do you think it works on me? I know what it means. You would like to be queen of this little dung-heap and the things that crawl in it. Any that manage to please you will get your other look for reward, eh? You make good use of your look. Well, we all use what we have. Even if we have nothing – a beggar can turn a profit from nothing. Enough. Enough of your look.'

The woman hurried to the bar and set the dish of food on it.

'You think I am bad? How would you, who are just an old peasant woman, know what is good and what is bad? Sometimes I think even God does not know.' Blanco took a swig of brandy. 'The question I ask myself: is Brother Kranz good? He is a man of position, people obey him . . . yet – in this world, did ever a good man rise? I do not know. I know I have a feeling in my heart for the man. But what does that signify? I had ever a ready heart. Please, give me a little of that meat, mother.'

The woman found a piece of salt fish in the stew and brought it in her fingers to Blanco.

144

'I have no money,' Blanco said. 'So I must beg. Julian the Hospitaller begged too. And wept so much it wore valleys in his face.'

Seventeen

The desert was always clean. Every day the wind swept it like a broom. So the footprints were not old. The wind blurred them even now and soon they would be gone. There was someone maybe half a day ahead. As the day ended the sun shone red through the dust-haze and the tracks that he could barely see at noon now stretched ahead as clear black dots on the crimson ground. When only half the sun's disc showed above the horizon he saw a big saguaro and the tracks led straight to it. Closer to, he saw the man. He was sitting underneath the giant fifty-foot cactus with his sombrero lowered to the setting sun. He knew him by his poncho. The man had been at the mission five days ago. The monks had fed him and given him a bed. As soon as he'd lain down on the bed he had fallen asleep, and the next morning early he had left without speaking to Ransome or to Nullo.

146

Nullo got down from his horse and the man looked up. Nullo stopped. Now that he saw him full face, he knew him. It was the farmer whose wife and daughter Blanco had murdered. But the farmer gave no sign he recognized him, so Nullo walked over and squatted beside him under the saguaro.

'I think you are going in the same direction as me.'

'I am going to the dunes,' Benito said.

'Me too. I will keep you company if you don't mind.'

'It's up to you. But as soon as I have rested my legs I am going to walk. I do not feel like sleeping tonight.'

'That is fine by me. You have business at the dunes?'

'Yes, I have business there. After I finish it I will sleep.'

Stars crowded the sky when they rode into the clump of shacks. They rode doubled up and Nullo could feel Benito's fear like you feel the thrum of a fading chord on a guitar.

'I know what your business is,' Nullo told Benito.

'Yes? You are clever.' Benito's voice was harsh and strained.

'I advise you to forget it.'

'Oh, yes? And what are you talking about?'

147

'Blanco. I know what he did to you.'

'Then you know why I have to do what I am going to do.'

'Blanco will kill you.'

'I have considered that.'

They climbed down from the horse outside the cantina.

'Listen to me,' Nullo said. 'I was there that day your wife and child were killed. I took no part in it, but I was there. Let me take care of this business with Blanco. You are a farmer, but me, I am a *pistolero*, so leave this work to me.'

'It took something to get my mind ready for this. Now my mind is ready. Ready to kill. I will kill Blanco or he will kill me – or I will take this rifle and kill myself.'

Benito walked to the door of the cantina. He pushed it open a few inches, then stopped. He stepped back and unslung the US Army issue Springfield from his back. The sound of the bullet going into the breech was loud enough to wake the dead, and if Blanco was in there, Nullo guessed he must be good and ready.

Sure enough, Blanco's voice came from inside:

'I am going to put a bullet through you if you walk in with that rifle levelled. But if you come in with it pointed at the ground, I will put down my pistol and we will see what is what.'

Benito lowered the Springfield then, and pushed open the door. Standing in the doorway, he blocked Nullo's sight, but from the way his head was turned, he could tell Blanco must be sitting somewhere along the left wall.

'Do you want something with me?'

'Señor Blanco, I have come to kill you.'

'Well, I am a fair man. There . . . my gun is on the table.'

Benito stood staring into the cantina. The sound of his breathing was loud and rapid. His right hand opened and closed, opened and closed on the stock of the rifle. Then his hand shut on the stock and tensed. His arm and his whole body tensed. The sound of his breathing stopped.

Nullo brought the gun-barrel down on Benito's head.

He holstered the Colt and stepped over Benito's body. Blanco smiled a slow smile. His gums looked very red against the white skin.

'Are you my guardian angel, Nullo?'

'Not hardly.'

Blanco's smile faded as slowly as it had come. 'Your gun is cocked. Be careful it does not go off.'

'Your gun's cocked too.'

Blanco's hand came an inch off the table. 'I would not want it to go off and hurt my friend. Let me uncock it, Nullo.'

'I ain't your friend, *cholo*. And when you go for that gun I'm gonna blow you to hell.'

Blanco lowered his hand to the table again. He lowered his head, and his left hand went to the rosary at his waist and fingered the beads. Nullo's fingers twitched beside the Colt's handle. Blanco raised his head.

'Why, Nullo?'

'I got my reasons. Same as you got your reasons for wearing that potato sack.'

'A man's reasons are very simple. That's what makes life such a dull business. You will be well quit of it.'

'Take more than a pink-eyed fish-belly like you.'

Blanco's mouth twisted. 'Don't try to make me angry. Your words mean no more to me than the whining of a mosquito. I have nothing more to say to you and I have forgotten your face already.'

Benito groaned. Nullo heard the rifle scrape on the boards. Blanco grabbed the pistol and Nullo jerked the Colt and fired.

Blanco's eye exploded like a raw egg hit by a hammer. His right eye blazed at Nullo and his finger pulled the trigger at the same instant that Nullo's palm fanned the hammer of the Colt. Three more slugs slammed Blanco out of his stool and the cantina shook as he hit the wall.

Nullo wiped a little fragment of Blanco from his cheekbone, and then, lowering his head slowly, he looked down at his own body. His buckskin shirt was splattered with blood, but he could see no hole. He resisted the urge to look round and see where Blanco's bullet had gone and, cocking the Colt, he tossed the table out of the way and went down beside Blanco.

Blanco's gun lay two inches from his twitching fingers. Nullo pushed it another foot away. There were three holes in the monk's habit. Blanco's right eyeball was moving, but you could see that Blanco didn't know where he was or who he was.

Nullo holstered his gun and picked up Blanco's. It was cold – and no smell of smoke from it either. He broke open the magazine There were five bullets in it and one empty chamber cylinder.

'What happened – slip your mind you weren't quite ready to shoot? *Pistolero* like you? Well ... guess a lot of people gonna be glad you're gone, but at least you won't be forgot in a while. That's just about as good as being mourned, huh, Blanco?'

At the sound of his name a spark of awareness gleamed in Blanco's eye. It was just enough to kill him. A rattle in his throat turned to a sigh and then his pale eye froze.

'You saved my life,' Benito said.

'Maybe not.'

'Oh, yes. I looked in Blanco's eyes and knew I would die. So, thank you.'

'Wait till that crow's egg parts your scalp before you thank me.'

'Your name is Nullo, no?'

'Well, let's just say it ain't Aloysius.'

'Eh? I speak no English. Jaime told me about you. Jaime Vargas. He told me what you did ... to Maria. . . .'

'He told you about that?'

'Yes, but . . . I believe I can understand the reason.'

'It takes a wise man to understand a man's reasons. Are you a wise man, Benito?'

'I am not very wise.'

'Well that's OK, maybe you don't need to be so wise. Blanco said a man's reasons are very simple, didn't he?'

Benito found Jaime under the big saguaro that he and Nullo had rested under. He stretched out beside him with his back to the saguaro and after a while he said:

'The albino is dead.'

'Good. That just leaves Nullo.'

'It was Nullo that killed him.'

Jaime looked at him. 'Nullo killed him?'

'And saved my life in the bargain. When he killed your wife, it was an act of mercy, Jaime. Maria was dead from the moment the white thing stepped through your door. You have Nullo to thank that she did not die as mine did.'

'Lame Deer foretold that I would kill Nullo and die doing it.'

'I think we are both meant to live and suffer more. But perhaps we can help each other in our suffering.'

Benito stood up. 'Come home, Jaime. Let us see what life has for us.'

'Ah, Benito, it is hard. But it helps to have a friend. So, dear Benito, help me to my feet. The pale pig is dead, eh? Oh . . . poor Maria . . . I miss her, Benito.'

Eighteen

The wind sighed over the dunes and skimmed a white mist off them. It sighed through Nullo's brain and swept the thoughts out of it. There was nothing to see but sand and nothing to hear but wind.

If Jaime Vargas's face and hair had not been white with dust, he might have just seen him on the ridge of a dune. Jaime lay stretched on his belly with a Winchester pointed at Nullo's heart. Lame Deer had said he would be like a rattler when it strikes, and Jaime found it was true. His mind was balanced like a hair on a pinhead. He could divide a second into twenty parts with the speed of his thought. He adjusted his aim by the width of a razor's edge and knew with a certainty it was true. He squeezed the trigger, and in the fraction of a second before it hit its mark, he watched the bullet glide through the air. Nullo fell

154

out of the saddle and all was as inevitable as the tick of time.

'Lame Deer was wrong, Nullo.'

The horse, which had stopped to look back, took fright and bolted again.

'He said I would kill you and you would kill me. But you're dead and I'm alive. Maybe it would have been more honourable to give you a fair fight. But I care as much about honour as I do about living. Are you there, Nullo? They say the ghost of a murderer hangs around. I had a talk with your one-armed friend – but I was forgetting, you have no use for friends. I thought I was your friend once. I suppose Blanco thought he was your friend too. Well, both of us were fooled.

'But I was saying, I spoke with your little gringo. He sends you his greetings. He is very pleased to hear that Blanco is dead. He remembers Blanco with some bitterness. It is only natural: there was not much of the little gringo to start with and Blanco reduced him even more. He is a man of some importance, your little gringo. Sometimes he eats with your president. He does favours for him too. The death of Blanco will please your president, I believe, because Blanco killed a cousin of his – a navy man whom your president loved well. I learned much from your little gringo – he was a little drunk because of the pain in his arm, and I think he will regret talking so much. He told me why you killed Blanco. He said he would obtain for you a pardon if you killed him. Benito was as disappointed as I. He thought you had saved his life out of the goodness of your heart. But it was just so you could claim your pardon. Well, your little gringo pardons you, but Jaime Vargas does not. I've served you your summons to appear before Lucifer post haste, and I hope he sticks a spit up your ass and grills you in hell fire, you dirty stinking sack of filth.'

Jaime wiped his eye, but it was because the dust bothered it, tears were a thing of the past. He slung his rifle and his canteen over his shoulder and began to walk.

Nullo raised his face out of the dust and saw Jaime Vargas walking away across the desert. It took him a few seconds to realize he'd been shot and that Jaime Vargas had shot him. The pain in his chest told him he'd been shot bad, and moving didn't help, but he reached to his holster and brought out his gun. He sighted between Jaime Vargas's shoulders and thumbed back the hammer. The wind, blowing in his eyes so he had to squint against the dust, drowned the sound of the gun cocking and Jaime Vargas did not look back. He squeezed on the trigger and the hammer drew back a little more until it wanted a feather's weight of pressure to slip its ratchet.

With his thumb he eased the hammer back against the pin and laid the Colt in the sand.

When Jaime Vargas was out of sight, Nullo put his cheek to the dust and closed his eyes.

The desert is as good a place as any for it, he thought. There's a desert where no cactus grows. Got to make a little trip there. It's just a question of sooner, or later. Never could make up my mind when I begun to think. I might bleed out nice and peaceful, but then again I might lie till the sun turns my head. The cards can have the say. Low card for the bullet, aces high. Six-spot or better says leave it lie.

Nullo eased the deck out of the breast pocket of his buckskin shirt. The pack was welded together and there was a hole through it. Right through one of the Jacks' faces. The tip of the bullet just broke through the bottom of the pack. He opened his shirt. His chest was bleeding and it was bruised red right across, turning blue at the armpits. He couldn't touch it to see, but he guessed his breast-bone was broken.

Might take longer than he thought. Could lie here a couple of days in the sun. It was a long walk to the next water-hole without a drink.

Well, I was in the army. Dogface ain't dead till he stops gripin'.

Nullo got a foot under him.

'Well, now. . . .'

He raised himself, tottered a little, but stayed on his feet.

Taught me how to walk in the army too.

157

'Keep the line, Mancini. You got two left feet, McFarlan?

'Step it out.

'What was the song the big mick Quincannon used to sing?

' "The first mate said 'Well, blow me down', and the captain said 'cor blimey'.

' "When I let them view the rare tattoo of the girl I left behind me. . . ." '

'Hup . . .

'Hup . . .'